THE LEGEND OF KORRA

ENDGAME

randomhouse.com/kids

ISBN 978-0-449-81734-6

Printed in the United States of America

10 9 8 7 6 5 4 3 2 1

nickelodeon

THE LEGEND OF KORRA

ENDGAME

Adapted by Erica David

Based on screenplays by
Mike DiMartino and Bryan Konietzko

Random House New York

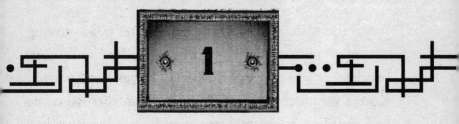

1

From a distance, Republic City looked every inch the bustling metropolis it was meant to be. The tall spires of skyscrapers and ornate pagoda towers created an impressive skyline unmatched in all the United Republic of Nations.

Founded by Avatar Aang over seventy years earlier, the city served as a beacon of hope. It was a place where benders and non-benders could live together in peace. People with the ability to control one of the four elements were known as benders, and those without this ability were non-benders.

Avatar Aang was no longer alive, but a giant statue of him kept watch over the city from a small island in Yue Bay. Each time Korra walked along the city's waterfront, she felt Aang's steady stone gaze. In the past, it had been a source of comfort for her. The Avatar was master of all four elements: water, earth, fire, and air.

It was the Avatar's responsibility to foster peace among the four nations—and between benders and nonbenders. It was a heavy burden on seventeen-year-old Korra's shoulders. As the current Avatar, she had come to Republic City to master airbending, but events had transpired to test her far more than she would have thought possible a few months earlier. . . .

Today, as Korra raced along the pier on the back of her polar bear–dog, Naga, Aang's gaze felt troubled. She knew it was impossible. The statue was mere stone, nothing more, but the city Korra was sworn to protect had been so damaged in the recent attack that she couldn't help imagining Aang's reaction. She was sure it would mirror her own.

Korra pulled Naga to a halt in front of Republic City's Pro-Bending Arena. The area was still roped off with yellow caution tape, and several Metalbender police officers patrolled the grounds, their black segmented armor making them look like insects in human form. Korra slid from Naga's back and let her gaze drift over the once-magnificent arena. Several of its tall spires were charred. The gilded glass dome that had been the arena's crowning glory was shattered. The jagged iron girders that had formed the dome's skeleton stuck out from the roof at odd angles, the metal gnarled and twisted.

Korra shivered as she took in the damage, and a cold feeling of foreboding crept over her. It had been less than a week since Amon and his Equalist revolutionaries had crashed through the dome at the Pro-Bending Championship Tournament. Amon's eerie masked face and raspy voice still haunted her nightmares. The vile Equalist leader and his henchmen had held the crowd captive in terror. Korra, her friends, and the police force had barely been able to force them back into the shadows.

And worst of all, she remembered the way Amon had demonstrated his ability to take people's bending power away. Only the Avatar could do that—or so she'd thought.

Korra blew out a deep breath and slipped beneath the caution tape. She darted toward one of the arena's side entrances and ducked into the building. It was odd being back inside. She hadn't set foot in the place since the night of the attack. There'd been a time when she'd looked forward to coming here every day for Pro-bending practice with her teammates, Mako and Bolin. Now the arena didn't feel so welcoming. It was as if the terror of that night had seeped into its walls.

Korra quickened her pace and tried to ignore the haunting echo of her footsteps as she hurried down an empty corridor. She kept to the outer halls, avoiding the building's interior, where the ruined stands and scorched remains of the Pro-bending ring brought unwelcome thoughts. That was where Amon had launched his Equalist revolution, declaring his intent to make the world "safe" for non-benders by stripping all benders of their abilities forever.

It's madness, Korra thought. Amon was tapping into the public's fear of people who are different from themselves and using it to drive a wedge between benders and non-benders! As the Avatar, it was her duty to protect those without bending abilities and promote harmony among all people.

Korra shook herself free of those worries and mounted the stairs to the top of the arena's tallest tower. Defeating Amon and his Equalists was going to be a daunting task, but luckily, she wasn't alone. She had her friends beside her, and one tiny piece of good news she couldn't wait to share with them.

At the top of the stairs, Korra pushed open the wooden door to Mako and Bolin's apartment. The brothers were in mid-conversation as they packed up their meager belongings.

"I still can't believe they're shutting this place down," Mako said.

"We made some great memories here, didn't we?" Bolin replied wistfully.

Just then, Korra stepped into the room. "Guys, great news! You don't have to go back on the streets. I talked to Tenzin and made all the arrangements. You can come live on Air Temple Island with me!"

Mako glanced at Korra, a smile beginning to tug at the corners of his mouth. The budding grin froze, however, and a flush heated his cheeks. He dropped his eyes. "We'd love to, Korra, but—"

"Asami already invited us to live with her in her dad's giant mansion!" Bolin blurted, easily excited as usual. "From here on out, it's the lap of luxury for us!"

Korra's face fell. She should have known Asami would offer to host the brothers. Mako was Asami's boyfriend, after all. It didn't matter how much Korra liked him.

She sighed and fought down the unsettling feeling she sometimes got when she thought about Asami. It would be easier if she could dislike Asami, but not only was Asami pretty and rich, she was also generous and kind. For all Korra's strength and fame as the Avatar, there were times when she felt she just couldn't compete with Asami—especially where Mako was concerned.

As if on cue, Asami's voice rang out from the loft above. "Hey, Korra! I was hoping you'd stop by." Stylishly dressed as always in a tight, dark jacket and a snug-fitting red dress, Asami climbed down the rickety wooden ladder from the loft. Bolin's pet fire ferret, Pabu, scrambled down after her and leapt to Bolin.

Korra pulled on her plain, fur-lined tunic. "I was just leaving," she mumbled, barely able to hide her disappointment. "So I guess I'll see you guys around sometime."

"Why not tomorrow?" Asami said brightly. "I'd love to have you come visit the estate."

"I don't know. I have some Avatar stuff to do."

"Oh, come on, Korra!" squeaked a tiny voice. Korra turned to see Bolin holding Pabu up like a puppet, throwing his voice to make the fire ferret talk. "We all deserve a little rest and relaxation after all this craziness. We can swim in Asami's pool. It'll be fun."

Korra chuckled. "All right, Pabu."

"Great. We'll see you tomorrow," Asami said.

Korra sighed and walked out the door, leaving Asami to help the brothers finish packing for their move to her palatial estate.

2

Across town, in front of Cabbage Corp's headquarters, Chief of Police Lin Beifong was busy engaging in her least favorite part of her job: fielding questions from reporters. Ever since Amon's attack on the arena, the mood in the city had shifted. Benders and non-benders regarded each other with skepticism and fear, and tensions were running high. There was increased pressure from the city council to bring Amon to justice, and the first step was for the police force to crack down on Equalist sympathizers.

"Is it true that Cabbage Corp is conspiring with the Equalists?" asked a reporter from the *Republic Daily News*.

"The evidence points in that direction, but the investigation is ongoing," Beifong answered.

Just that morning, she'd led a special team of Metalbender police officers on a raid of one of Cabbage

Corp's automobile factories. Once inside, they'd discovered all sorts of Equalist propaganda pamphlets and posters, but the strongest evidence had been in the form of a secret stash of weapons. Beifong remembered the anger she'd felt as she ripped open a wooden crate on the factory floor, revealing row after row of the electrified gloves used in Amon's attack. It was more than enough evidence to arrest Lau Gan-Lan, the head of Cabbage Corp.

A flurry of flashbulbs popped and crackled, drawing Beifong back to the present. Police Captain Saikhan emerged from the foot of the glimmering Cabbage Corp office tower, pushing an indignant Lau Gan-Lan in front of him. The CEO struggled against the thin metal cables that bound his hands behind his back. His silver mustache worked furiously as he cried, "This is an outrage! I'm innocent!"

Beifong ignored him and turned back to the crowd of reporters in front of her. "For the time being, we have frozen Mr. Gan-Lan's assets and are closing Cabbage Corp."

"No! Not my Cabbage Corp!" Gan-Lan shrieked as Saikhan ushered him into a waiting police vehicle.

Chief Beifong looked on with grim satisfaction. The arrest was a small victory in the battle against Amon, but it would do little to relieve the pressure from the

city council. They'd already called for her resignation—
or rather, Councilman Tarrlok had. He blamed her for
failing to stop the attack on the arena.

Tarrlok had been angling to have Beifong dismissed
ever since he'd discovered he couldn't keep her under
his thumb. The crafty councilman clearly intended to
replace her with someone he could easily control.

Tarrlok was right about one thing, however: Lin
Beifong had failed, and now Republic City was in
grave danger. But no one could blame her more than
she blamed herself.

Pro-bending champion Tahno was the last person
Korra expected to see when she walked into police
headquarters. She was due to meet with Chief Beifong
and Tenzin, her airbending master and mentor, but
they were nowhere in sight. In fact, the lobby of the
grand building was empty save for the occasional
Metalbender officer clomping across the glossy marble
floors in heavy armored boots.

Ordinarily, Tahno would have been surrounded by
a gaggle of adoring fans and hangers-on, but today the
charismatic former captain of the White Fall Wolfbats
Pro-bending team sat alone on a stone bench. His hair,

usually perfectly coiffed, looked thin and bedraggled. He sat with his shoulders hunched, his hands hanging limply between his knees.

"Hey, Korra," Tahno said listlessly.

"Tahno?" Korra was startled by his appearance. She hadn't seen him since the Pro-bending championships just before Amon's attack, when he and the Wolfbats had cheated their way to victory over her team, the Fire Ferrets. He'd always been cocky, overconfident, and all-around arrogant. She hated to see him so diminished—another victim of Amon's terrifying ability.

Korra sat down next to him on the bench. "Listen, I know we're not exactly best friends, but I'm sorry Amon took your bending."

The thought of it sent a shiver down her spine. She could see it all over again in her mind's eye: the way Amon loomed over his victims, forcing them onto their knees, fixing them with that hollow-eyed stare through the slits in his pale, menacing mask; then the grip of his clawlike hands and the rasp of his gloved finger against their foreheads as he stripped their bending away. It had nearly happened to Korra once, but Amon had spared her at the last moment, deciding to leave their confrontation for another day.

Tahno straightened his shoulders and drew himself

up to look Korra in the eye. "I've been to the best healers in the city," he said. "Whatever Amon did to me, it's permanent."

Korra could hardly believe this was happening. How was someone other than the Avatar able to take away people's bending? Perhaps the Spirits really had turned their backs on her. After all, she'd never made contact with her past lives as the Avatar. Maybe she wasn't worthy to carry the title. Maybe the Spirits of her past lives did not want to make contact with her as Amon had said.

"You gotta get him for me," Tahno said with some of his former fierceness.

Korra swallowed hard and nodded.

Just then, the sound of footsteps interrupted them. Korra turned to see Tenzin and Chief Beifong approaching with Asami's father, the inventor and wealthy industrialist Hiroshi Sato, who was promising that if he remembered anything more about the Equalists, he would tell them.

Korra nodded politely to Mr. Sato. She knew him well because he had sponsored her Pro-bending team.

Tenzin beckoned Tahno. It was his turn to be questioned.

Tahno gave Korra a final glance and smirked, looking

more like the pompous, self-centered Waterbender he used to be. She grinned when he teased, "See you around, *Uh*-vatar."

At least he still had his ego.

3

The expansive estate of Hiroshi Sato was an intimidating sight. A large gray stone mansion dotted with tiered towers and shimmering glass windows sat amid several acres of rolling green hills. The property extended as far as the eye could see and included guesthouses, stables, and an inventor's workshop.

A butler greeted Korra at the front door when she arrived and guided her through the mansion's cavernous halls. Sato's stately home was as lavish as his daughter Asami was stylish, with beautifully furnished rooms and expensive works of art. The humble lodgings on Air Temple Island could not compare.

The butler led Korra into a sprawling indoor courtyard that housed a huge heated pool. Bolin and Pabu backstroked contentedly at one end while

Mako and Asami splashed each other playfully. Korra grimaced. They looked happy.

"Avatar Korra!" the butler announced.

Bolin stopped midstroke and turned to Korra. "Welcome to paradise!"

"Looks like you guys have settled in," Korra said wryly.

"Pretty much," Mako replied. He cut his eyes to Asami. "Except someone forgot to ask her father if we could stay here."

Hiroshi Sato had already been generous, as far as Mako and Bolin were concerned. He'd sponsored the Fire Ferrets in the Pro-bending championships with money from his highly successful company, Future Industries.

Asami shrugged at Mako and gave him a pretty smile. "Yeah, but I smoothed it over with him," she said. "It's easier to ask for forgiveness than permission."

Bolin paddled over to the side of the pool and hopped out next to Korra. He could barely contain his excitement. "This is the greatest place in the world!" he cried. "Watch this!"

He snapped his fingers, signaling the butler. "Fetch me my towel, good sir."

"Yes, Master Bolin," the butler replied, stone-faced.

"'Master Bolin' . . . I love this guy!" Bolin grinned. "Now pat me dry."

"As you wish," the butler replied. He pulled a fluffy white towel from over his shoulder and began to buff Bolin vigorously.

Korra chuckled. Clearly, Bolin had adjusted to living in the lap of luxury with no problem whatsoever.

Asami swam to the edge of the pool to speak to Korra. "I'm glad you made it," she said cordially. "Do you want to come in?"

"Nah, I'm all swum out. I sorta swam here from Air Temple Island."

"Wow. In that case, let's move on to the next activity," Asami suggested.

"What'd you have in mind? Shopping? Makeovers?" Korra asked halfheartedly. The Avatar couldn't think of anything more boring than an afternoon spent shopping with Asami.

"Oooh, I vote makeovers!" Bolin answered, clasping his hands together wistfully.

Asami climbed out of the pool and started to towel herself dry. "Actually, I had something a little more exciting planned."

15

Korra leaned forward in the outdoor grandstand at the largest racetrack she'd ever seen. A winding black strip of road lined with bright red and white barriers snaked through a wide swath of perfectly manicured grass. Sleek racing Sato-mobiles streaked over the asphalt at record speeds, engines roaring and fenders glinting in the afternoon sun.

Asami, Mako, and Bolin sat in the empty stands next to Korra, eagerly following the action on the track below.

"Pretty cool, huh?" Asami asked, noting the look on Korra's face. The Avatar's mouth hung open in astonishment.

"Way cooler than a makeover," Korra agreed.

"This is where Future Industries test-drives their Sato-mobiles," Asami explained. "Ever been behind the wheel?"

"The only thing I know how to drive is a polar bear–dog," Korra admitted.

"Want me to take you for a spin?"

Korra raised her eyebrows in surprise. She glanced over at Asami, who was elegantly dressed, as usual. The daughter of Republic City's most famous industrialist looked like she was about to go to a fancy dinner at Kwong's Cuisine, not hop behind the wheel of a hot rod. Still, Korra was excited.

"Let's do it!" she said.

Asami stood and headed down the steps of the grandstand with Korra close on her heels. When the two of them reached the racetrack below, a grease-stained mechanic greeted them. He helped Asami suit up in a sleek leather racing jacket and handed both girls helmets and driving goggles.

A shiny yellow Sato-mobile was brought onto the track for Asami. Korra marveled at the vehicle's design. Its glossy, torpedo-shaped body sat low to the ground, balanced on wide-set rubber tires. The top of the hot rod was completely open, with tandem seating in the cockpit.

Asami jumped into the driver's seat and Korra climbed in behind her. They pulled up to the starting line alongside a test-driver in a bright red sports model. He drew his goggles down over his eyes, ready to race. Asami glanced at him and revved the engine confidently. Korra grinned. It was just like psyching out opponents at a Pro-bending match.

The mechanic stood on the side of the track, holding a checkered flag in the air. He dropped his arm, swirling the flag with a flourish. Asami reacted quickly, stomping the accelerator to the floor. She and Korra sped from the starting line. The race was on.

4

Engines roared. The test-driver took an early lead, cutting in front of Asami on the straightaway. She wasn't about to let him keep that lead. She gripped the wheel and dug in, shifting gears to urge the hot rod faster. The tires screamed over the asphalt, churning up dust. Wind whipped against Korra's face, carrying the faint scent of burning rubber. She leaned forward in the passenger seat, absolutely exhilarated.

The two vehicles took the first curve in a squeal of tires, hugging tight to the inside of the track. As they came out of the turn, Asami saw an opening. She whipped the wheel to the right, determined to pass the red Sato-mobile on the outside, but the test-driver caught sight of her and drifted to the right as well, narrowing the lane and effectively blocking her path. Asami had no choice but to let up or run the risk of a collision. She eased the car into a lower gear and backed off her opponent's bumper.

Both vehicles slowed slightly to take a sharp curve. This time, Asami was ready. As soon as the track straightened, she downshifted, trading speed for power, and cut to the inside of the red hot rod. The test-driver wasn't at all fazed by her gutsy move. He responded with a bold move of his own, ramming the side of Asami's car so that she was wedged between him and the side of the track.

Sparks flew as the driver's side of the yellow Satomobile grated against the metal guardrail. Korra gritted her teeth and gripped the front of her seat, fearing they were headed for a crash. But Asami maneuvered deftly and, with a burst of acceleration, rocketed into the lead. She streaked across the finish line and brought the vehicle to a skidding halt.

The two girls leapt out of the hot rod, victorious.

"That was amazing!" Korra said, tearing off her helmet and goggles. "I didn't think we'd make it."

Asami grinned. "Well, you can't be afraid to mix it up sometimes."

Korra was impressed. She didn't even think Asami knew how to drive at all, let alone drive like *that*. She'd just assumed such a wealthy family would have a chauffeur.

"I gotta admit, I had you pegged wrong," Korra confessed. "I thought you were kind of prissy. Uh, no offense."

"It's all right," Asami laughed. "People usually assume I'm Daddy's helpless little girl, but I can handle myself. I mean, I've been in self-defense classes since I was a kid. My dad made sure I would always be able to protect myself."

"Smart guy," Korra replied. She looked at Asami with grudging admiration. It occurred to her that maybe the two of them weren't so different. After all, they both knew how to handle themselves. Was it possible they could actually become friends?

Later that afternoon, Korra stared into an enormous gilt-framed mirror that hung in the second-floor powder room at the Sato mansion. The room was bigger than her entire living quarters on Air Temple Island, and its opulent fixtures twinkled in soft, warm light. A dizzying array of beauty creams and cosmetics lined the counter in front of her. She glanced down at them suspiciously.

Korra tried to tell herself that fancy face paints and flowery perfume were responsible for Asami's hold on

Mako, but even as she thought it, she knew it wasn't true. Asami had proved herself to be more than just a pretty face today.

Korra reached out, her fingers skimming the lids of the tiny porcelain jars and crystal vials assembled before her. At last, they settled on an ornate ceramic pot, its surface bathed in shimmering decorative enamel. She lifted the lid of the dainty pot and peered inside. It was full of pale, loose powder that sparkled when it caught the light.

She looked from the powder pot to her reflection in the mirror. Korra didn't see how the sparkly dust would change anything. It wouldn't transform the color of her clear blue eyes or alter the thin, dark slash of her brows. It couldn't change her dark brown hair, which she usually wore pulled back, except for the slim, banded locks that framed her face in the traditional Southern Water Tribe style. Still, she was curious.

Korra picked up a fluffy round puff from the counter and dipped it into the pot until its fibers were thoroughly coated in shimmering powder. Before she could talk herself out of it, she clapped the puff squarely against her face. A huge cloud of sparkly dust flew into the air. It traveled straight up her nose and into her mouth. She sneezed and coughed, dropping the offending puff.

When the dust settled, Korra stared into the mirror again. She looked exactly the same except for a blotch of pale powder coating her nose. She scrubbed it off and gave her reflection a rueful smile. There was no escaping her features, and that was perfectly fine with her.

She was the Avatar; she didn't need a makeover.

On her way back from the powder room, Korra got lost on the sprawling second floor of the Sato mansion. Mako, Bolin, and Asami were waiting for her in the first-floor foyer, but she must have taken a wrong turn somewhere. A long, dark hallway stretched before her with doors at regular intervals on either side.

Korra noticed that one of the doors on her left was slightly ajar and heard a voice coming from the other side. She walked over to the door, thinking she could ask for directions, but what she heard made her stop short.

"No, no. I assure you. Everything is going exactly as planned." It was Hiroshi Sato, Asami's father. "Well, lucky for you, the Cabbage Corp investigation has bought us some time."

Korra peered into the room through the open door.

Sato was a portly man in his fifties with a distinguished look about him. He sat behind a huge wooden desk covered in papers. His thick, graying mustache rode the curve of his upper lip as he spoke into a telephone.

"Trust me. By the end of the week, we'll be ready to strike."

Korra stiffened. Sato's words sounded ominous.

Cabbage Corp was being investigated for ties to the Equalist movement, but she couldn't see how that would benefit Sato—unless he was the one actually working for Amon. A chill crept up her spine, and the tiny hairs at the back of her neck stood on end.

Korra backed away from the door and hurried down the hall, convinced that Hiroshi Sato wasn't what he appeared to be.

5

That night, Korra met with Tenzin and Chief Beifong on the roof of police headquarters. After overhearing Sato's conversation, she'd left the mansion abruptly. She knew her friends were puzzled, but something had to be done right away.

"So you think Mr. Sato is building weapons for the Equalists, and framed Cabbage Corp?" Tenzin asked Korra. His brow was furrowed, scrunching the lines of the pale blue arrow tattoo that began at the base of his shaved head and came to a point just above his eyebrows. The Master Airbender and son of the previous Avatar, Aang, stroked his beard in thought.

"That's a bold accusation, but what proof do you have?" asked Chief Beifong.

"Well, I don't exactly have proof, but I know what I heard. Sato's up to something," Korra said.

"He does have the means." The chief of police mulled it over. "And he has a motive."

"That's right," Tenzin agreed.

"A motive? What is it?" Korra asked.

"Twelve years ago, the Agni Kai Triad robbed Sato's mansion. They killed Sato's wife during the break-in," Tenzin explained.

"That's terrible," Korra murmured.

"It was tragic," Tenzin said with a sigh. "It's possible he's been harboring anti-bending sentiment all this time."

Chief Beifong nodded her agreement. "Maybe we should look at Mr. Sato a little more closely."

The Sato mansion gleamed in the early-morning sunlight. The grounds were quiet at this time of day, so when Korra rang the bell, accompanied by Tenzin and Chief Beifong, the resounding chime echoed loudly across the rolling green hills of the estate.

After several moments, the butler answered the door and ushered the three of them inside. At the request of Chief Beifong, he agreed to take them to see Hiroshi Sato in his upstairs study. As the group headed toward the grand staircase leading to the second floor, Mako and Asami walked into the foyer. When they caught sight of the police chief and the serious expression on

Tenzin's face, Mako crossed to Korra and pulled her aside.

"What's going on? What do they want with Hiroshi?" he asked.

"I . . . overheard him on the phone yesterday," Korra said haltingly. She turned to Asami, who had just walked over to join the two of them. "Asami, I don't know how to tell you this, but I think your father might be involved with the Equalists."

Angry, Asami narrowed her eyes. "I don't believe this!" She spun on her heel and ran to the stairs, headed for her father's study.

Mako scowled at Korra and her heart sank. "You spied on Hiroshi?" he asked incredulously. "What's your problem?"

Before she could attempt to explain, Mako turned his back on her. He stalked off after Asami, leaving Korra no choice but to follow.

"Mr. Sato, we just have a few follow-up questions for you," Chief Beifong said, her eyes moving carefully around the study in search of anything out of the ordinary.

Hiroshi Sato sat behind his elaborately carved

wooden desk. The surface was cluttered with what looked like plans for one of his latest inventions. He rose from his chair, calmly considering the chief and Councilman Tenzin, who stood at her side. He was just about to reply when Asami stormed into the room.

"My father is innocent! Just because we're not benders doesn't mean we support those awful Equalists!"

Mako and Korra walked into the study in time to catch the tail end of Asami's outburst. They watched as she stood beside her father, facing Tenzin and the chief with a defiant stare.

"Equalists? Is that what this is about?" Mr. Sato asked. "I can assure you I have nothing to do with those radicals."

Mako folded his arms across his chest and glowered at the Avatar. "Yeah, you don't know what you're talking about, Korra."

"I overheard you on the phone," Korra said to Mr. Sato. "You said the Cabbage Corp investigation bought you time and you're getting ready to strike. Explain that!" She didn't want to hurt Mako or Asami, but she knew what she'd heard. Her instincts told her that something wasn't right.

Hiroshi Sato met Korra's gaze with a hard stare, but it quickly dissolved as he chuckled softly. "This is all just a misunderstanding resulting from the young

Avatar's overactive imagination. My number one competitor was knocked out of the game. It's providing me an opportunity to strike the market with a new line of Sato-mobiles."

Chief Beifong looked over at Tenzin, the two of them weighing Sato's answer. The Master Airbender wasn't entirely convinced.

"In order to put all suspicions to rest, might we have a look into your factories and warehouses?" Tenzin asked.

Asami gasped, outraged, but Sato raised a hand to silence his daughter.

"If you feel it's necessary, you're welcome to search all of Future Industries," he replied.

Chief Beifong nodded curtly. If Hiroshi Sato was hiding something, they'd be sure to find it.

Future Industries had several factories and warehouses located throughout Republic City. It took Chief Beifong and her Metalbender officers the better part of the day to search all of them. Tenzin and Korra joined the effort, working alongside the police to strip open cargo crates and inspect storage containers. Even Korra's polar bear–dog, Naga, took part in the search, using her keen sense of smell to sniff out anything unusual.

It was dusk when the police finally finished their inspection of the last warehouse. Despite Korra's suspicions, they'd found no incriminating evidence whatsoever. The huge wooden crates that lined the walls of the facility were filled with ordinary Sato-mobile parts. There were no hidden rooms or secret weapons stashes, no posters of Amon's frightening masked face. There was nothing to link Hiroshi Sato to the Equalists.

Outside the warehouse, Korra stood with Tenzin and Chief Beifong, watching as the last of the Metalbender police force filed out of the building empty-handed. The officers discharged the metal cables hidden in their armor and used them to latch on to the police airship hovering above the building. As they retracted their cables, they were reeled up into the gondola of the ship.

Once the officers were inside, the huge black zeppelin with its pointed metal fins banked slowly. Korra could hear the powerful whir of the ship's propellers as it turned and floated off toward police headquarters.

"I can't believe we didn't find anything," she said.

"It would appear Hiroshi is innocent," Beifong admitted. The police chief let out a heavy sigh. Even though there was no evidence against Mr. Sato, something didn't feel right to her.

Mako and Asami approached Chief Beifong. Asami had insisted on being present during the search. She wanted to be there when her father was cleared of suspicion.

"Okay, you did your search," she said. "Now you can all leave."

Beifong gave Asami an annoyed look, but she knew the girl was right. She and Tenzin withdrew, and Mako took Korra aside.

"I hope you're convinced now," he said, dropping his voice to a whisper.

"No, I'm not," Korra replied stubbornly. "I don't care how cooperative Hiroshi is being. I know he's lying."

Mako plowed a hand through his spiky black hair, agitated. His dark eyes glittered with anger. "Why are you doing this? Are you that jealous of me and Asami?"

"What?" Korra spluttered. Her eyes widened in surprise, then quickly narrowed. "Don't be ridiculous! That has nothing to do with it."

"If you don't drop this, consider our friendship over," Mako warned.

Korra stared at him, her eyes softening with her

own hurt feelings. "I'm sorry, but Hiroshi is not the man you think he is."

Exasperated, Mako sighed and stalked away. He went back to Asami, who was waiting nearby, and the two of them walked off. Korra refused to watch them. It would only make the lump in her throat that much harder to swallow.

Instead, she turned toward Naga. The enormous polar bear–dog sat back on her haunches just a few feet away. Korra crossed to her best friend and reached up to scratch the thick fur behind her ears.

She was deep in thought a few moments later when a warehouse worker bumped into her. Korra turned from Naga, startled. The man bowed his head in apology. He backed away quickly, but not before he shoved a folded scrap of paper into her hand.

Korra called after the mysterious man, but he hopped into a waiting cargo vehicle and disappeared. Curious, she turned her attention to the paper. She unfolded it and scanned the cramped handwriting.

"I think you guys should see this," she called to Tenzin and Chief Beifong. As soon as they approached, she read the note aloud. "'If you want to find the truth, meet me under the north end of the Silk Road Bridge at midnight.'"

Korra exchanged a glance with Tenzin and the chief of police. It was an appointment they planned to keep.

The Silk Road Bridge was one of the marvels of Republic City. Made of sturdy iron girders the color of burnished brass, the suspension bridge connected two of the city's largest boroughs. At this time of night, its tension cables were dotted with light, making it visible to airship pilots from a distance. Korra waited anxiously beneath one of the bridge's huge support towers along with Tenzin and Chief Beifong.

At the stroke of midnight, she heard a whisper. "Psst. Over here."

Korra turned to see the warehouse worker who'd slipped her the note. He wore a cap pulled down low over his eyes, and the collar of his jacket was flipped up to keep anyone from recognizing him. He slipped out of the shadows and approached the three of them. The man looked around nervously before he began to speak.

"Listen, I joined the Equalists because I believed in what Amon said. I thought he could make life better for us non-benders. But I didn't sign up for this . . . this war."

"What do you have on Hiroshi Sato?" Beifong asked.

"He's manufacturing those gloves for the Equalists, and there are rumors he's working on something even bigger, some new kind of weapon," he explained.

Korra released a breath. She knew Sato was up to something! Now, finally, someone was backing her story. She only wished Mako was hearing this, too.

"We searched all of Future Industries and found nothing," Tenzin said.

"That's because he has a secret factory."

"Where?" Korra asked.

"It's right underneath the Sato mansion." The warehouse worker bowed quickly. He'd said all he had to say. He tucked himself farther into his coat and slipped off into the night.

Tenzin looked over at Chief Beifong, practically seeing the wheels turning in her mind as she formed a plan. He knew what she was going to do.

"Raiding the Sato mansion is a risky move with Tarrlok breathing down your neck," Tenzin said. "If we're wrong . . ."

"I know. I can kiss my job goodbye." Beifong sighed. "But protecting Republic City is all I care about. We can't let Amon get his hands on this new weapon."

6

The police airship broke through the thin clouds of the night sky, hovering just above the Sato mansion. On board, Korra and Tenzin peered through the glass windows of the gondola at the huge estate below. Across from them, Chief Beifong faced a troop of Metalbender officers standing at attention. She signaled to the airship's pilot, and moments later, the bay doors at the rear of the gondola slid open.

The officers jumped through the opening, attaching the metal cables hidden in their armor to the sides of the ship. As the cables unspooled, the Metalbender police lowered themselves to the ground. The elite team of troops struck out across the estate, taking Sato's guards by surprise.

The raid on the Sato mansion had begun.

Asami, Mako, and Bolin were enjoying a quiet evening in the den when the heavy wooden doors burst open. Metalbender police swarmed into the room. Their shiny black armor clanked menacingly as they surrounded the three teenagers.

"What are you doing here?" Asami screamed. Bolin screamed, too, but an octave higher.

Chief Beifong marched in after the last of her officers. Tenzin and Korra followed.

"We have reason to believe there's a factory hidden below the mansion," Beifong explained.

"I think I would have noticed if there was a factory underneath my house!" Asami snapped. "Honestly, the lies you people come up with just to persecute my father."

Tenzin stepped forward. "Where *is* your father?"

"In his workshop behind the house," Asami said grudgingly. She shot Tenzin a bitter look.

Chief Beifong signaled to her officers and they filed out of the room, headed for the workshop. Asami followed them. She was determined to prove once and for all that her father was innocent.

Hiroshi Sato's workshop was a low, squat building located just behind the main house. He often went there in the evenings after dinner to work on his new inventions. Asami fully expected that tonight would be no different. When the Metalbender police kicked in the doors of the workshop, they'd find her father at his workbench tinkering with his latest prototype.

Instead, the workshop was empty. The lights were on, and there were tools and machine parts scattered around, but there was no sign of Hiroshi.

Mako and Bolin stood with Asami as the police inspected the room. Tenzin and Korra joined the search, but in the end, the result was the same. Hiroshi Sato was nowhere to be found.

At last, a Metalbender officer stepped forward to report to Chief Beifong. "Chief, the estate has been secured. No one's left the workshop since we arrived."

Beifong looked carefully at her surroundings. Sato had clearly been in his workshop earlier, but he wasn't here now. There had to be another way out, something her eyes had missed.

"Perhaps we just couldn't *see* him leaving," she said. The police chief, a Master Earthbender, turned her focus to the armored boot on her right foot. The boot's metal casing warped under her intense gaze and bent away to reveal her bare foot. She closed her eyes and slammed her foot down on the floor, her earthbending power causing a small tremor.

Beifong stood completely still as a series of sound waves pulsed from her foot. The waves traveled through the earth, their vibrations painting a picture only she could read. Beifong's mother, Toph, blind since birth, had seen the world this way. Both Toph and Beifong used earthbending as an extension of their senses.

After a moment, the chief of police opened her eyes and metalbent her boot back into place. "There's a tunnel beneath the workshop, running deep into the mountainside," she announced.

"What? There's no tunnel," Asami argued.

Beifong ignored her. She thrust her hands out and raked the air, causing a huge sheet of the workshop's metal floor to buckle. With a quick twist of her hands, she tore the sheet up and tossed it against the far wall. The gaping hole in the floor revealed the entrance to a secret tunnel.

Asami reeled in disbelief. "I—I don't understand," she stammered. "There must be an explanation." Mako placed a comforting hand on her shoulder.

Korra walked over to the two of them. It was clear she'd been right about Hiroshi, but she wasn't happy to see Asami upset. "Maybe you don't know everything about your father. I'm sorry," she said softly.

Asami turned away, unable to look Korra in the eye.

Chief Beifong ordered her officers to proceed into

the tunnel. A closer look revealed a wide staircase that led down into the darkness. The Metalbender police started down the stairs with Beifong, Tenzin, and Korra bringing up the rear. Asami, Mako, and Bolin tried to follow, but the police chief insisted they remain behind under the watchful eyes of her trusted lieutenant, Officer Song. There was no telling what they would find at the end of the tunnel, and the chief refused to put innocent people in danger.

The tunnel ran deeper than anyone expected. When the group finally reached the bottom, the passage opened up into a huge underground factory. Power turbines and other manufacturing equipment were set up along the outer edges of the room. A twisting network of pipes and ducts lined the walls, and the high ceilings were crosshatched with metal beams. Two large cloth banners hung from a beam in the center of the room. Amon's masked face stared out from them, rippling across the fabric.

"Not your average backyard workshop," Beifong said.

"And I'm guessing those are the new weapons," Korra murmured in awe.

Her eyes came to rest on Sato's latest invention, an armored suit nearly fifteen feet tall that was a dangerous blend of machine and metal monster. The mechanized robot had jointed arms with clawlike pincers for hands. At the bottom of its thick, trunklike legs were rubber treads instead of feet, allowing the machine to roll forward and crush anything in its path. The head of this metal beast was an armor dome dotted with round glass windows. With the largest window in the center, glinting like a single threatening eye, it looked almost like a deep-sea diving helmet.

The mecha-tanks were lined up in rows of three, facing each other from opposite sides of the factory floor. Korra shivered. If Amon got his hands on these weapons, there was no telling what kind of damage the Equalists could do.

"Hiroshi was lying, all right," Tenzin said, breaking the silence. "But where is he?"

At the sound of Tenzin's voice, a massive metal wall slid down from the ceiling. It crashed to the floor with a loud clang, sealing off the passage that led to the tunnel. Korra and Tenzin exchanged worried looks. They were trapped.

7

"What was that?" Bolin asked.

He was waiting in Hiroshi Sato's workshop with Asami and Mako under the vigilant gaze of Officer Song. The Metalbender policeman was humorless. He had barely let them move an inch.

"We need to get down there and see what's going on!" Mako insisted at the sound of the loud bang coming from the secret tunnel.

"Absolutely not. You're staying put until the chief comes back," the officer replied.

Mako glanced at Bolin. The brothers traded knowing looks before Mako turned back to Officer Song.

"All right, we'll stay put. But can we wait outside or something? It's so dusty in this workshop," Mako complained.

Asami arched an eyebrow. The first time she'd met

Mako, he'd been coming home from a shift at the Republic City power plant covered in soot. It would take more than a little dust to bother the Firebender. Clearly, he was up to something.

"No. We're waiting right here," Officer Song said firmly.

"Okay, but don't blame me if I start sneee . . . if I start sneeeee . . ." Mako's voice broke off as he pretended to stifle a sneeze. His hands fluttered in front of his nose and his eyes began to water.

"What's your problem, bub?" Officer Song's patience was wearing thin.

"I'm about to . . . I'm gonna . . . *AH-CHOO!*" Mako lurched forward with the force of his sneeze and a bright burst of flame shot from his mouth. Startled, Officer Song reared back. Bolin took advantage of the distraction to bend the earth upward. Mako shoved the policeman and sent him tumbling.

In a matter of seconds, Mako and Bolin tied the officer's hands up with a nearby power cord and stuffed a gag into his mouth.

"Sorry, pal," Mako apologized. "We know you were just doing your job."

"Yeah, you just stay put until the chief comes back," Bolin said. "That sounds very familiar, doesn't it? Why? Because you said it."

Pleased with himself, Bolin started for the entrance to the tunnel. Mako followed close behind. He stopped when he saw Asami move to come with them.

"Asami, you should stay here. We'll check it out," Mako said.

Asami bit her lower lip, troubled. "I have to find out the truth about my father."

"I understand. That's why I'm going down there for you. Please." Mako held her gaze a moment, his eyes steady.

Asami considered his words and took a deep breath. After a minute, she agreed. "Be careful, Mako," she said, brushing a tear from the corner of her eye.

Chief Beifong had been in worse scrapes. The gleaming metal wall that closed off the tunnel to Hiroshi's workshop presented little obstacle for a Metalbender. She ran toward the wall, focusing her thoughts, channeling her energy to send it crumbling to the ground.

She struck out with earthbending force. The wave of power shot from her body and rocketed toward the wall, slamming against the surface with a sound like a resounding gong. But then the unexpected happened.

The wave rebounded, sending Beifong staggering back. The wall stood untouched, not even a dent in its surface. Somehow, it had repelled her attack.

Impossible! she thought.

Korra gasped in disbelief and Tenzin's eyes widened in shock. The Metalbender officers were equally astonished. They closed ranks around the chief, enclosing her in a protective circle.

Suddenly, an amplified voice cut through the silence.

"I'm afraid you won't be able to metalbend that wall, Chief Beifong. It is solid platinum." The voice belonged to Hiroshi Sato. Korra spun around, trying to figure out where the voice was coming from. Her question was answered, however, as the mecha-tanks on either side of the room lit up, a spooky pale green glow emanating from their round glass portholes. There was no question—Sato was inside one of the mechanized suits.

"My mecha-tanks are platinum as well. Not even your renowned mother could bend a metal so pure," the inventor taunted. The six robo-suits began to roll forward, their metal plates vibrating with the hum of hidden engines.

"Hiroshi, I knew you were a lying, no-good Equalist!" Korra shouted. "Come out here and—"

"And do what, young Avatar? Face the wrath of your bending? No, I think I'll fight from inside here, where my odds are a little more *equal*."

The mecha-tanks advanced, pressing the group back toward the platinum wall.

"That source was a setup!" Beifong said. She thought back to the meeting under the Silk Road Bridge and how easily the warehouse worker had given up the location of the secret factory. "You lured us here!"

"Guilty as charged," Hiroshi replied.

All at once, the mecha-tanks leveled their claws with a pneumatic hiss. The Metalbender officers leapt into action, lashing out at the tanks with the metal cables from their uniforms. The cables looped around two of the mecha suits. The police tightened the cables, trying to topple the battle suits or pull them apart.

The metal-plated robots struggled, their hydraulic arms caught in the cables and bound to their platinum bodies. The struggle was short-lived, however. Electricity burst from the robo-tanks. The current crackled down the length of the metal cables, electrocuting the officers on the other end. Three officers dropped to the ground, unconscious.

With a startled cry, Tenzin, Korra, and Beifong joined the fight. The Master Airbender slashed his arms through the air in a spiraling arc that summoned powerful gusts of wind, then sent blasts of air at the tanks.

Korra stomped the ground, earthbending the factory floor. The concrete cracked and buckled. She raised the broken chunks of mortar and hurled them at the advancing mechanized suits. The sharp fragments only bounced off the platinum-plated tanks, doing little to slow their process.

Chief Beifong and her three remaining officers turned their attention to the metal ducts and equipment lining the edges of the room. They bent pipes and turbines, grinding the metal into razor-sharp pieces of shrapnel. The police launched the shrapnel at the robo-suits, hoping to pierce their platinum armor. The mecha-tanks slowed momentarily under the hail of metal fragments, but their armor remained impervious to the attack. Within moments, they advanced as if nothing had happened. The tanks' heavy rubber treads rolled over the debris, flattening it with the ease of a team of steamrollers.

When the officers fell back to regroup, the Equalist operators inside the tanks took advantage of the temporary retreat. In unison, the tanks lurched to a stop and the pincers of their robotic claws ratcheted open. Each claw launched a two-pronged grappling hook at the end of a long cable. The hooks struck the three Metalbender officers and clamped shut around them. In a matter of seconds, the cables flared with electricity, shocking the officers and knocking them unconscious.

Chief Beifong also found herself clenched in the cold iron grip of a grappling talon. But before the sizzling sparks of electricity could reach her, she used her bending to warp the metal gauntlets of her armor, transforming them into shiny blades with the wicked sharpness of swords.

Beifong sliced through the grappling hook's cable, freeing herself just in time to escape electrocution. She snarled as she rounded on the tank closest to her, running directly into its path. They were about to collide, but at the last possible moment, Beifong kicked against the cement ground, creating a tremor. The rumbling earth launched her high into the air.

The police chief landed on top of the oncoming mecha-tank, using her gauntlet blades to slash through the glass eyes of the machine's metal dome. She heard an alarmed cry from the cockpit and peered through one of the portholes. Hiroshi Sato squirmed out of the way of the chief's blades, frantically jerking the tank's control levers.

You're mine, Sato, Beifong thought. She had just

reared back to plunge her blades into the cockpit again when another tank's grappling hook locked on to her from behind. The tank operator wasted no time flooding the cable with current. Beifong's body shook as the shock coursed through her. She reeled and fell off the top of Sato's robo-suit, tumbling to the ground with a thud.

From the corner of his eye, Tenzin saw the police chief go down. He and Korra had been keeping the tanks at bay as best they could, but they barely managed to slow them down. Tenzin pounded away with a barrage of air strikes, while Korra unleashed the full wrath of her earthbending. She rattled the machines by tearing ruts in the ground beneath their treads and continued to pelt them with shards of rock. Tenzin covered her when he could, blasting the machines back toward the walls with gale-force gusts of air.

He was too late, however, to protect Korra from the grappling hook that suddenly arced across the room and closed around her. It slammed the Avatar into a turbine at the edge of the factory floor and knocked her unconscious.

"Korra!" Tenzin shouted. He summoned a pocket of air and surfed its crest, zigzagging through the machines and their treacherous claws. The Airbender's anger bubbled to the surface. He sent fierce winds whipping through the space and managed to knock over one of the mecha-tanks.

The remaining tank operators still had plenty of tricks up their sleeves. One of the armored suits leveled a claw and launched a spinning metal disk from between its pincers. As the disk flew toward Tenzin, it ejected electrified bola cords. The weighted cords whipped through the air, gaining momentum. Tenzin tried to evade them, but they slammed into his body. The electrified bands closed around him and emitted a high-voltage shock. He lost consciousness and crumpled to the ground.

With their opponents defeated, the mecha-tanks ground to a halt. The metal chest plates of the tanks swung open, and Hiroshi Sato and his men climbed down out of the cockpits. Among the men stood a tall, imposing figure whose face was half concealed behind a pair of antique brass goggles and a mask. The lower part of his face was exposed, revealing a black mustache. The sleek hair hung down on either side of his lips like fire ferrets' tails. Belted at his waist were two electrified kali sticks. He was Amon's lieutenant and second-in-command.

Hiroshi Sato nodded to the Lieutenant before he

turned to survey the unconscious bodies of his enemies on the factory floor.

"Well, I'd say that was a near-flawless test run," Sato said, grinning. He motioned to his men. "Load everyone into the transports. Deliver them to Amon."

8

When Mako and Bolin reached the end of the underground tunnel, they found it sealed off by a huge metal wall. The muffled sounds of a fight leaked through from the other side. Bolin's stomach dropped. Whatever was happening on the other side of that wall couldn't be good.

Desperate to discover what was going on, the brothers decided to tunnel beneath the wall. As the Earthbender in the family, it was up to Bolin to create a passage. He focused his thoughts on the task of hollowing out the ground beneath his feet.

Slowly but surely, the brothers burrowed under the wall. When they surfaced at last, Bolin lifting away a chunk of concrete in a dark corner of the factory floor, they were shocked at the scene before them.

Korra, Tenzin, and Chief Beifong lay unconscious

on the ground, and the rest of the Metalbender officers were being loaded into cargo trucks.

"Oh no," Bolin whispered.

"Korra was right," Mako said. "We gotta do something, quick!"

The brothers climbed through the hole in the floor and crept into the shadows. They worked their way carefully around the edge of the room until they drew close to Korra and Tenzin. Mako hoisted Korra's body over his shoulders while Bolin freed Tenzin's arms from the bola filaments. He stooped and drew the unconscious Airbender onto his back.

"Not so fast, boys."

Mako and Bolin looked up to see Hiroshi Sato and the Lieutenant blocking their escape. The Lieutenant drew his kali sticks from his belt. He twirled them easily in his hands, ominous sparks dripping from the tips of the batons. Hiroshi brandished weapons of his own. He raised his hands, which were covered in heavy, elbow-length gauntlets. Electricity coursed through the gloves.

"Hello, Mr. Sato," Bolin said, his voice deceptively cheery. "Wow, this is a really swell factory you have here under your mansion."

Mako didn't feel much like joking. He narrowed his eyes, glaring at the famous inventor. "So sponsoring our Pro-bending team, supporting the Avatar . . . it was all just a big cover."

"Yes," Hiroshi admitted, "and the most difficult part was watching my daughter traipse around with a firebending *street rat* like you."

Hiroshi flexed his gloved fingers, causing streaks of lightning to ripple between his palms.

"Dad, stop!" a voice demanded.

Everyone turned to see Asami standing next to the hole in the floor. Unbeknownst to Mako and Bolin, she'd followed them. Not one to wait around, she had just climbed in and was now staring in horror at her surroundings. From the Equalist propaganda banners to the dangerous mecha-tanks, Asami couldn't believe her eyes. This ugliness. This hatred. This was . . . her dad?

Slowly, she walked toward her father, tears streaming down her cheeks. "Why?" she asked brokenly.

"Sweetie, these people, these benders, they took away your mother, the love of my life," Hiroshi explained. "They've ruined the world! But with Amon . . . we can fix it and build a perfect world together. We can help people like us everywhere!"

Korra stirred on Mako's back. Her eyes blinked open in time for her to see Asami's expression flatten.

"Join me, Asami," Hiroshi said. He stripped off one

of his electrified gloves and held it out to his daughter.

Asami's eyes grew glassy and cold. She took several halting steps toward her father and then lifted the glove from his hands.

"No!" Mako gasped in disbelief. He watched Asami draw the heavy gauntlet onto her arm.

Hiroshi smiled, pleased with his daughter's choice. Asami took one long look at Mako and then turned to her father. "I love you, Dad," she whispered sadly.

Suddenly, she turned the glove on Hiroshi, blasting him with a bolt of electricity. His eyes widened in surprise as the current struck him. He dropped to the floor, unconscious.

Realizing Asami had betrayed her father, the Lieutenant rounded on her, kali sticks blazing. She spun quickly and danced beyond his reach, grabbing one of the sticks with her glove. Lightning shot out from the electrified rod, but Asami redirected it, sending the bolt back at the Lieutenant. His body jerked as he fell to the ground.

"Let's get out of here!" Mako shouted. Hiroshi's men were climbing back into the mecha-tanks. They had only a few moments to escape.

Bolin roused Tenzin and the two of them pulled Chief Beifong safely to the hole in the floor. Mako, Korra, and Asami followed. As Asami climbed into the tunnel, she took one last, heartbroken look at her father. She sighed heavily as Bolin bent the earth over the tunnel entrance to protect their escape. Despite Hiroshi's twisted thoughts, he'd done one thing right: he'd raised her to be able to protect herself. Now, on her own, she would have to.

Inside the gondola of the police airship, Asami stared through the windows. The Sato mansion faded into the distance as the ship pulled away. She wrapped her arms around herself as if she were cold.

Mako watched her from a few feet away and then turned to Korra, who was standing next to him.

"I'm sorry I didn't believe you," he said, lowering his eyes. "But Asami's dad being an Equalist is not an easy thing to believe. Even now."

"I know," Korra replied gently. "I'm sorry this whole thing happened."

"So, does your offer to live at Air Temple Island still stand?" he asked.

"Of course it does. And Asami is welcome, too."

"Thank you so much," he said.

Korra put her personal feelings for him aside. "After

everything she's been through, she's going to need you, Mako."

Mako nodded firmly. He walked over to Asami and put his arms around her. She dashed the tears from her eyes and buried her face in Mako's chest. Even though Korra still had feelings for Mako, she knew Asami needed him more right now. Without her father, Asami would need friends. Korra made up her mind to do her best to be a good one.

Chief Beifong and Tenzin stood near the ship's engine room, deep in discussion.

"My Metalbenders are on their way to Amon, and it's my fault," Beifong growled. The six officers had been loaded into Sato's cargo trucks. There hadn't been time to rescue them from the secret factory. "I led them right into another trap."

Tenzin shook his head. The chief of police was being far too hard on herself.

"Councilman Tarrlok is right to call for me to step down. First thing in the morning, I'm handing in my resignation."

"Lin, you can't give up like this," Tenzin said.

"I'm not giving up. I'm going to find my officers and take Amon down, but I'm going to do it my way—outside the law." Chief Beifong pulled the small gold badge from the chest plate of her shiny black armor and pressed it into Tenzin's hands.

Troubled, the Master Airbender closed his fingers around it.

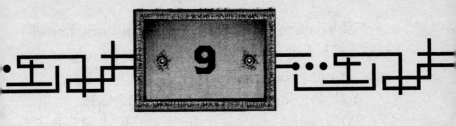

Air Temple Island was in the middle of Yue Bay, not far from the giant stone statue of Avatar Aang. It was home to Tenzin; his wife, Pema; his daughters, Jinora and Ikki; and his son, Meelo. Korra had come to live with them to complete her airbending training along with the other Air Acolytes under Tenzin's instruction. Over the past few weeks, she'd come to know every tree-lined path, training ground, and animal habitat on the island.

Korra stood at the end of a long pier and watched as a sailboat crewed by Air Acolytes arrived. Next to her, Jinora, Ikki, and Meelo fidgeted in their red and gold Airbender's robes. They couldn't wait to welcome their new guests.

Soon the acolytes tied off the boat and lowered the gangplank. Mako, Asami, and Bolin emerged and stepped onto the dock. Pabu scrambled after them.

"Welcome to Air Temple Island, your new home!" Ikki cried. Tenzin's middle child was eager to give the new arrivals a tour.

"Yes! Welcome to my domain!" said Meelo.

"Well, aren't you sweet, little monk child," Bolin said, chuckling. He and Mako each carried a small satchel of belongings. Asami, on the other hand, had a number of heavy trunks and packages. The Air Acolytes in the sailboat's crew struggled to unload them.

"Thanks for sending the Air Acolytes to help us with the move," Mako said to Korra.

"No problem. Everyone here wants you to feel welcome," she replied.

Korra led the group from the docks onto a twisting path sheltered by trees. The kids surrounded the new guests as they walked, with Meelo next to Asami.

"You're pretty!" Meelo blurted. "Can I have some of your hair?"

Asami smiled, flattered, and Mako laughed. "Looks like I have some competition."

Ikki raced out in front of the group to point out some of the island's more interesting sights. "The flying bison sleep in those caves down there, and that's the temple Grandpa Aang built, and that's the greenhouse where we grow the vegetables we eat."

"I have a few questions," Bolin said. He rattled off a list, speaking almost as quickly and as excitedly as Ikki had. "Is this an all-vegetarian island? Is that where you train airbending? Do we have to wear Air Acolyte clothes? Do we each get our own sky bison? And, final question, how many trees are on the island?"

Ikki answered without skipping a beat. "Yes, yes, no, no, one thousand five hundred fifty-two."

Satisfied, Bolin nodded.

"So where are we going to be staying?" Mako asked.

"You're a boy. Boys have to stay on the boys' side," Meelo answered.

Jinora, the older daughter, sidled up next to Mako. "I'd be happy to show you to the men's dormitory!" she gushed.

"Meelo, why don't you go with the boys, too?" Korra said. "Ikki and I will take Asami to the girls' side."

The group split up at the end of the path, where Meelo bowed and said goodbye to Asami with a flourish. "We shall meet again soon, beautiful woman."

Korra and Ikki showed Asami to the women's living quarters. Ikki chattered nonstop the whole way there.

For the most part, it was harmless information about the island, but as Korra turned into Asami's room, Ikki spilled an embarrassing secret.

"Asami, did you know Korra likes Mako?"

Korra blushed, horrified. She wanted to scream, die, run and hide, and shout that it was true all at the same time. But mostly she wanted Ikki gone. Far away.

"Oh, uh . . . no, I wasn't completely aware of that," Asami stammered in shock.

Korra's face stung with embarrassment. She grabbed Ikki by the sleeve of her robes and dragged her out into the hall. "Run along, Ikki!"

She gently pushed the precocious girl away and stepped back into the room with Asami, slamming the door.

An awkward silence settled between Korra and Asami. The Avatar shifted her weight nervously from foot to foot before she finally spoke, changing the subject.

"So . . . here's your room. I know this is a little rustic compared to what you're used to."

"I think it's really charming," Asami said. "And the best thing about it? Nothing here reminds me of my father. Thank you for your hospitality."

Just then, they were interrupted by a gentle knock on the door.

"I said run along, Ikki!" Korra snapped.

Instead of Ikki, it was Tenzin who opened the door. "Good day, ladies. Asami, welcome to the island."

"Thank you for having me," she replied.

Tenzin nodded and turned to Korra. "Beifong's replacement, Saikhan, is going to be inducted as the new chief of police later today. I think we should both be there."

Korra nodded in agreement. Republic City was going to be a different place without Beifong as the chief. It was time to find out just how different.

10

The newly installed Chief Saikhan was a decent man who'd served under Chief Beifong for many years. As he addressed the press and the public on the front steps of police headquarters, it was clear he was dedicated to bringing Amon and his Equalists to justice.

Crafty Councilman Tarrlok made Korra suspicious. He was standing way too close to the new chief, like a puppet master afraid of losing his grip on the strings.

Korra's suspicions were confirmed when Saikhan announced he'd be reporting directly to Tarrlok on all matters concerning the Equalist revolution. The Metalbender police force was a separate branch of city government. No chief had ever reported to a council member.

"What is that weasel-snake Tarrlok up to now?" Korra whispered to Tenzin as the press conference drew to a close. Tenzin sighed heavily in response.

As the crowd dispersed, Tenzin and Korra made their way toward the steps of police headquarters, intercepting Tarrlok.

"Tarrlok, I don't know what you did to get Chief Saikhan in your pocket, but I highly doubt it was legal," Tenzin said.

"Oh, Tenzin, always the conspiracy theorist," Tarrlok replied smoothly. His expensive silk robes and neatly oiled locks gleamed in the late-afternoon sun. "Did you ever consider that Saikhan simply recognizes my talents and wants what is best for this city?"

Tenzin snorted but refrained from rolling his eyes. It would have been unbecoming for a councilman, not to mention a Master Airbender. Instead, he folded his arms across his chest and harrumphed.

Tarrlok greeted Korra with an unusually warm grin. "Well, Avatar Korra, long time no see. Now that your little Pro-bending distractions have run their course, I look forward to your return to my task force."

"Forget it. There's no way I'm rejoining your vanity project," Korra muttered.

Tarrlok had created a special task force of Metalbender officers to track down the Equalists. He'd goaded Korra into joining, but it hadn't lasted long. She'd quickly recognized the task force as yet another one of Tarrlok's attempts to gain power.

Tarrlok shrugged at Korra's refusal. "That is unfortunate to hear. But I am sure you will come to your senses, as you have in the past."

"Don't hold your breath, bub," Korra said. "You know, Tenzin's been right about you all along. You played me, you played Beifong, and now you're playing the new chief, too. Well, I got news for you—you need me, but I don't need you. I'm the Avatar."

Tarrlok smiled calmly, a glint in his eye. "You are not, in fact, the Avatar. You are merely a half-baked Avatar-in-training. Which reminds me, how *is* your airbending going? Made any *significant* progress with that?"

Tarrlok's words stung. Airbending was the weakest of Korra's abilities. No matter how hard she trained, she couldn't seem to master it. She stared at Tarrlok, speechless with anger and humiliation.

The councilman gave her a mocking bow. "If you will not be a part of my task force, then you had best stay out of my way."

Tarrlok's threat lingered in the silence that followed. At last, he turned his back on Korra and Tenzin and strolled confidently into police headquarters.

"I don't understand what's wrong with me," Korra said glumly. She sat huddled in the back of Oogi's saddle while Tenzin sat comfortably just behind the neck of the flying sky bison, guiding the enormous creature with his reins. Oogi coasted slowly through the clouds, his shaggy white-and-brown fur ruffling in the breeze.

"I've memorized all the practice forms, but I still can't produce a single measly puff of air! I'm a failure!" Korra moaned.

"No you're not. You just need to work through this airbending block," Tenzin advised.

"Amazing advice. I'll get right on that."

"I wasn't finished yet. You see, Aang had not only his bending teachers, but also his past lives to call upon for guidance. Have you ever made contact with your past lives?" asked Tenzin.

Korra shook her head. The spirit of the Avatar had been reincarnated once every generation since the beginning of time. She should have been able to reach out to the Avatars who had come before her. "No, of course I haven't. Didn't you get the memo? I'm a spiritual failure, too."

"You may have made a connection without realizing it. Perhaps something you mistook as a dream?"

Korra frowned, deep in thought. When Amon

had captured her and knocked her unconscious, she'd seen a blur of confusing images. "Maybe . . . I've had a few weird hallucinations, but I hardly even remember them."

"Did you see any of the previous Avatars in these visions?" Tenzin prodded.

"I saw Aang." Korra sat up straight, suddenly remembering. "It seemed like he was in trouble. What do you think it means?"

Tenzin stroked his bearded chin. "Hmm, I don't know, but I urge you to meditate on these visions. I believe Aang's spirit might be trying to tell you something."

Korra sighed, thinking about the last time she'd tried to meditate. It hadn't gone very well. If meditation was the answer to unlocking her full potential as the Avatar, then she was in a world of trouble.

The sun was setting over Air Temple Island when Mako, Asami, and Bolin set out to look for Korra. No one had seen her since she and Tenzin returned from Chief Saikhan's press conference. She'd even missed dinner.

Bolin had enlisted the help of Pabu to track her

down. The three teenagers followed the fire ferret as he sniffed and darted along the island's winding paths. Finally, at the top of a steep incline, Pabu chattered excitedly.

Bolin peered into the distance and saw Korra sitting on the very edge of a rocky outcrop with her back to them. Her shoulders hitched up at the sound of their approach.

"There you are!" Bolin said. "Hey, are you okay?"

"I'm fine," Korra said in a muffled voice. She climbed slowly to her feet and turned around. It was clear from her expression that she wasn't fine. Dried tear tracks streaked her face.

"Come on, what's wrong?" Mako asked gently. "You can tell us."

Korra took a deep breath. "How am I supposed to save the city when I can't even learn airbending? I'm the worst Avatar ever. I just feel . . . alone."

"That's nonsense. You're amazing!" Asami said.

"Yeah," Mako agreed. "And remember, Aang hadn't mastered all the elements when he was battling the Fire Nation. He was just a little kid."

"And he wasn't alone. He had his friends to help him," Bolin said exuberantly. "Look, the Pro-bending Arena might be shut down, but we're still a team. The new Team Avatar!"

Mako, Asami, and Bolin huddled up next to Korra, just like a Fire Ferrets' huddle before a Pro-bending match. Bolin stuck his hand into the center of the huddle, and everyone else followed suit. Korra couldn't help but smile. The team spirit was contagious.

"Let's do it!" she said.

Suddenly, a small bundle of squirming arms and legs draped in red and gold airbender's robes leapt from the bushes nearby and landed on top of everyone's hands. Meelo giggled with excitement.

"Yeah, let's do it!" he squeaked. "Wait, what are we doing?"

The new Team Avatar laughed, but Korra realized it was a good question. If they were going to work together to save the city, there were a few things they needed to figure out.

11

It was dark by the time Korra walked Naga into the stone courtyard at the base of the Air Temple. Mako and Bolin were already waiting for her, and when she arrived, Bolin let out a whoop of excitement.

"Get ready, Republic City. You are about to be patrolled by Team Avatar!" he declared. At Bolin's enthusiastic words, Asami joined them. She'd changed into the leather racing jacket she'd worn at the Future Industries test course and put on the electrified glove she'd taken from her father.

"Asami, you always know how to accessorize your outfits," Mako said, grinning.

"I figure one way to fight Equalists is to use an Equalist weapon," she replied.

Korra looked over her team, feeling confident. Republic City was in good hands. "All right, let's ride!" she said.

Team Avatar scrambled onto Naga's back in a tangle of elbows and knees.

"Naga away!" Bolin cried.

Naga's saddle sagged under the weight of the four teens. The polar bear–dog howled in complaint. Korra inched forward to make more room for the others behind her, but it was too late. The saddle was already sliding off Naga's back, taking the team with it. In a matter of seconds, everyone tumbled to the ground.

"All right, scratch that," Korra said, climbing to her feet. "Any other ideas?"

Asami looked thoughtful. "Hmm, I think I have the answer."

The convertible hot rod cruised through the streets of downtown Republic City. Borrowed from the Future Industries test track, it was midnight black with a shiny chrome grille and exhaust pipes that gleamed under the streetlamps. Asami sat behind the wheel with Mako next to her in the passenger seat. In the backseat, Bolin and Korra scanned the streets, on the alert for any sign of Equalist activity.

"I gotta say, I like the new Team Avatar's style," Mako said.

"No doubt about it," Bolin agreed. "This is the best way to patrol the city."

Asami reached out and flipped a switch on the dashboard. The radio crackled to life. "My dad had police scanners installed in all his cars. I guess now I know why."

Korra leaned forward as the police dispatcher's voice blared through the speakers.

"Calling all units, level-four alert. Jailbreak at headquarters. Officers down, electrocuted. Chi-blockers and Equalist convicts still at large, armed and dangerous. Last seen heading east. I repeat, level-four alert—"

The broadcast was cut off by the sound of squealing tires up ahead. Four masked Chi-blockers on motorcycles sped into the intersection, flanking a large cargo truck full of escaped prisoners. Chi-blockers were the most dangerous and highly trained among Amon's henchmen.

Korra's eyes widened. This was just what Team Avatar had been waiting for.

"Let's get 'em!" she shouted.

Asami was quick to react. She punched the accelerator to the floor and peeled out after the escaped Equalists in hot pursuit.

The hot rod's engine roared as Asami shifted gears and closed in on the motorcycles. She weaved in and out of the other cars on the road, most of which pulled to the side to avoid being sideswiped by the vehicles in the high-speed chase.

The Chi-blockers were expert riders, zigzagging across the road and cutting through narrow alleys. Asami kept pace, easily maneuvering the sleek Sato-mobile through hard turns and tight corners.

The chase spilled out onto an empty boulevard, a straight shot along the border of the Dragon Flats borough. Asami sped up, urging the car even faster in the straightaway. She was rapidly gaining ground on the fleeing Equalists.

Suddenly, a large truck pulled across the street up ahead, cutting her off from the Chi-blockers. Team Avatar was headed for a collision.

"Korra, Bolin, give me a ramp—now!" Asami shouted.

Bolin and Korra leapt into action, leaning out over the sides of the hot rod to earthbend the road in front of them. The ground rumbled and a tall ramp made of rock sprang up directly in front of the Sato-mobile's whitewall tires. Asami accelerated just in time. The car launched off the top of the ramp and flew beyond the truck.

Moments later, the hot rod landed, its tires and suspension howling. Asami downshifted, regaining control of the vehicle, and then pressed forward once again. This time, the four Chi-blockers and their motorcycles were within firing distance.

Mako gripped the top of the windshield for balance and stood up in the front seat. He drew back and hurled a bolt of blue lightning directly at the nearest Chi-blocker. The bolt hit the rear tire of the enemy motorcycle, causing it to spin out and skid into a parked car.

With one rider down, the rest of Team Avatar went on the offensive. Bolin leaned out from the backseat, churning up a storm of disks from the road's surface. He sent the shards of earth whirling toward the remaining riders, pelting them mercilessly. The masked Chi-blockers swerved to avoid the barrage of dirt and rock, but one of the riders was unsuccessful. Several disks nailed him squarely between the shoulders. He fell from his bike, tumbling to the ground.

The last two riders hunched low over their motorcycles and released dark clouds of smoke from the rear of their bikes. The thick smoke cut visibility down to almost nothing. Korra, Mako, and Bolin squinted into the fog, but Asami was ready. She pulled on a pair of driving goggles and caught sight of the Chi-blockers as they guided their bikes into a sharp right down a narrow street.

"Help me out!" Asami yelled. "We gotta make this turn!"

Korra stood up in the backseat, earthbending a curved ramp for Team Avatar's vehicle. Asami jerked the steering wheel hard to the right and the hot rod tilted dangerously as it sped onto the incline. The black Sato-mobile took the corner and leveled out with a thud as it left the ramp.

Asami slapped a lever on the dashboard, switching off the hot rod's headlights.

"They don't know we made the turn," she said. "Get ready."

Asami gunned the engine and the hot rod burst through the dense cloud of smoke, ramming the two motorcycles from behind. The Chi-blockers leapt from their seats and somersaulted onto the hood of the hot rod seconds before their bikes toppled and fell beneath the wheels of the car.

Mako launched himself forward in the front seat, shooting a burst of flame at the Chi-blocker in front of him. Amon's henchman dodged the fiery attack and managed to snare Mako's wrist in a bola cord. Mako yanked his wrist back, trying to drag the Chi-blocker over the windshield into the front seat. The masked man resisted and trapped Mako's other wrist with a second bola. With both wrists tied, Mako grappled with the rider, unable to launch another flame burst.

Meanwhile, the other Chi-blocker cartwheeled over the windshield and landed squarely in the middle of the car. The masked woman rounded on Korra and Bolin in the backseat and wasted no time mounting her attack. She aimed a series of precise strikes at the pressure points in Bolin's arm. He howled in pain and then in anger as his arm went numb. She'd blocked the chi coursing through his body, the energy he used to earthbend.

The Chi-blocker turned to Korra and was about to strike when Asami took her gloved hand from the wheel and wrapped it around the woman's ankle. Asami triggered the glove, zapping the masked rider with a bolt of electricity. The Chi-blocker collapsed into the backseat, unconscious.

With the Chi-blocker out of her way, Korra was clear to help Mako, who was still struggling with the rider on the hood of the car. She grabbed Mako and hauled him into the backseat, dragging Amon's henchman over the windshield. Asami moved quickly, zapping the Chi-blocker with her Equalist glove. He slumped down into the backseat.

Now that the Chi-blockers had been defeated,

Asami turned her attention to the cargo truck full of prisoners. She sped forward, rapidly closing in on the vehicle.

Mako freed his wrists and stood up in the backseat of the Sato-mobile. Balancing carefully, he leaned forward and leveled a bolt of lightning at the truck. The lightning hit the center of the truck's rear bay doors and crackled over the surface of the vehicle. The truck swerved unsteadily, tires squealing, and tipped over onto its side. It was several moments before the heavy vehicle finally skidded to a stop.

Asami pulled over to the side of the road and Mako and Bolin leapt out of the hot rod. They followed Korra over to the truck just as its rear doors fell open. The escaped prisoners were slumped over inside, unconscious but unharmed.

Team Avatar had already finished tying up the Equalist prisoners by the time the Metalbender police arrived. The officers were led by Councilman Tarrlok and his special task force. A flurry of reporters followed in their wake, eager to get the scoop on the jailbreak.

Tarrlok scowled as he looked over the scene. His

frown deepened when he spotted Korra and her team guarding the captured prisoners.

"Avatar Korra, what do you think you're doing?" he hissed angrily.

"Oh, hey, Tarrlok," Korra said nonchalantly. "Nice of you to show up finally. We captured the escaped convicts for you."

"What you did was tear up the city and impede the real authorities in pursuit of these criminals."

"That's funny. I didn't see your little task force or the cops the whole time. If it wasn't for Team Avatar, they would've gotten away."

Tarrlok took a step forward and leaned down so that he was glowering directly into Korra's face. "This is your last warning. Stay out of my way!" he growled.

Korra stared back at him calmly. After a beat, Tarrlok turned on his heel and stalked off into the night.

12

Team Avatar's first ride was such a success that they took to patrolling the streets regularly. Tonight, the team was parked on a narrow street in downtown Republic City. Korra, Mako, Asami, and Bolin leaned casually against the black racing Sato-mobile, eating take-out noodles and listening to the police scanner.

So far, the night had been quiet, but Korra was feeling uneasy. Just that afternoon, Tarrlok had passed new legislation in city council requiring all non-benders to be inside their homes by nightfall. Tenzin objected to the law on the grounds that it punished all non-benders for the actions of a few Equalists. He'd tried to convince the three other council members to vote against Tarrlok's plan, but he'd been outnumbered.

Glancing at Asami, Korra knew there was at least one non-bender out after nightfall tonight. Of course, the curfew wasn't a law that Team Avatar cared to obey.

"All available units, please respond to the fifty-six hundred block of the Dragon Flats borough." The police dispatcher's voice crackled over the airwaves. "Equalists have taken to the streets. Consider them armed and dangerous. Proceed with caution."

The team jumped to attention. Asami hopped behind the wheel, and Bolin slid in next to her. Korra bolted the rest of her noodles and turned to climb into the back of the car. Mako was already there. He gave her a polite bow and opened the door for her.

"After you," he said. He flashed her a charming grin.

"What a gentleman. Thanks," Korra replied. She hopped into the backseat and Mako settled in next to her. Neither of them saw Asami watching them intently in the rearview mirror.

When they arrived in the Dragon Flats neighborhood, the first thing Korra noticed was that the power was out. The streets were completely dark except for the roving spotlights from police airships overhead.

Soon a large crowd came into view. Metal barricades set up by the police were holding them back. Metalbender officers patrolled the barriers, keeping a close watch on the angry crowd.

Asami slowed the hot rod to stop just outside the line of Metalbenders. Team Avatar climbed out, ready for action, but a closer look at the crowd brought them up short.

"Wait a second—these people aren't armed or dangerous," Asami said.

Korra let her eyes move over the people behind the barricades. They weren't Equalist thugs or masked Chi-blockers. They were ordinary men, women, and children. "Sure doesn't look that way," she agreed.

Just then, Chief Saikhan's voice blared out into the night. He was standing among the officers at the barricade, addressing the citizens through a megaphone. "All non-benders return to your homes immediately!"

There was an angry rumble from the crowd.

"Yeah, as soon as you turn the power back on!" a man shouted.

"Disperse or you will be arrested!" Saikhan warned.

"You benders can't treat us this way!" said a woman standing just inside the barrier. She hugged her daughter close. The girl couldn't have been more than eight years old. Frightened, she held on to her mother tightly. Her eyes wandered over the line of police officers and came to rest on Korra.

"Mommy, look, it's the Avatar!" the girl said.

"Please, help us!" the woman yelled. She waved desperately to Korra. "You're our Avatar, too."

Korra took the woman's words to heart. She was right. The Avatar's duty was to protect benders and non-benders alike.

"Everyone please stay calm!" Korra called to the crowd. "I'm gonna put a stop to this."

She scanned the ranks of the Metalbender officers by the barricade and spotted Tarrlok and his task force. She should have known the councilman was behind this injustice.

"Tarrlok!" Korra shouted. She marched over to him, the rest of Team Avatar falling in behind her. "You need to turn the power back on and leave these people alone!"

"Avatar Korra, you and your playmates have no business here," Tarrlok said, annoyed.

"We're not going anywhere. You don't have the right to treat these innocent people like criminals."

"This is an Equalist rally. There is nothing innocent about it," the councilman snarled.

Asami spoke up. "They're not Equalists. They're just normal people who want their rights back."

"*They* are the enemy!" Tarrlok whirled around to face the Metalbender police. "Round up all these Equalists!"

The officers responded at once, breaking the barricades apart and metalbending the iron rails around groups of frightened people. Next, the police stomped their boots on the ground to earthbend a rolling tremor. The road surface rippled beneath the panicked citizens and erupted into broken chunks. The jagged slabs of ground rumbled and began to rise into the air. Innocent people shrieked as they found themselves floating on chunks of rock. The Metalbender officers guided the floating rocks toward the police transport vehicles, effectively capturing the so-called Equalists.

Korra sprang into action, striking out at the air with her hands and then drawing them sharply downward. The swift motion gently lowered the floating chunks of rock to the ground. The Metalbender officers were undaunted. They unleashed their metal cables, capturing anyone who tried to escape.

Angered by Korra's attempt to thwart him, Tarrlok lashed out with a water whip. The plume of water wrapped around Asami's wrist.

"Hey! Let me go!" she shouted.

"You are under arrest," Tarrlok hissed.

"What? You can't do that!" Mako said, running toward Asami.

"Actually, I can. She's a non-bender out past curfew, and her father is a known Equalist conspirator," the councilman said smoothly.

"Let her go!" Mako roared.

Tarrlok narrowed his eyes, considering, and then turned to the police. "Arrest him—and his brother!"

The Metalbenders launched their cables and wrapped them tightly around Mako and Bolin.

"Tarrlok!" Korra shouted. She kicked up two huge slabs of earth, challenging the councilman to make the next move. The police stood at the ready, poised to turn their metal cables on the Avatar.

"Unless you want to join your friends in prison, I suggest you put those down and go back to the Air Temple," Tarrlok warned. His eyes glittered with malice.

"Korra, listen to him," Mako said calmly. "It's not worth it."

"We'll be all right," Bolin assured her.

Grudgingly, Korra dropped the slabs to the ground. She could only watch helplessly as Mako, Bolin, and Asami were led to the police transports.

"Don't worry," she told her friends. "I'll call Tenzin. He can get you out!"

Tarrlok fixed Korra with an exceedingly smug grin.

"So sad to see your little 'Team Avatar' broken up. You had a good run."

"This isn't over, Tarrlok!" Korra snapped.

"Oh, I believe it is," he purred menacingly.

13

The lobby of police headquarters was crowded with Metalbender officers and people taken into custody at the Dragon Flats raid. Tenzin pushed his way through the crowd, desperate to find Korra. He spotted her at last, pacing anxiously in front of the station's information desk.

"I came as fast as I could. Are your friends all right?" he asked.

"I don't know. These knuckleheads won't tell me anything!" Korra groaned in frustration.

"I'll take care of this," Tenzin said. He stepped up to the counter and leaned forward to get the attention of the officers working there.

At that moment, Chief Saikhan walked past. He saw Tenzin and tried to duck away, but the Master Airbender was too quick for him. "Saikhan, a word."

The chief let out a heavy sigh and faced Tenzin reluctantly.

"Councilman Tenzin, I'm pretty swamped. Can this wait?"

"No, it cannot. Three of Avatar Korra's friends were wrongly arrested tonight. I'd like you to release them immediately." Tenzin pinned Saikhan with his steady gaze.

"They're not going anywhere. They were interfering with police business."

Korra bristled. "Your so-called police business was rounding up innocent people and claiming they were Equalists. They should be released, too!"

"All the Equalist suspects are being detained indefinitely," Saikhan explained. "They'll be freed if and when the task force deems they are no longer a threat."

"Those people are entitled to due process under the law," said Tenzin.

"You'll have to take that up with Councilman Tarrlok." The police chief shrugged. He was following orders.

"Oh, I plan to," Tenzin said evenly. "At the council meeting, first thing in the morning."

Korra couldn't contain her anger. She pushed in front of Tenzin and stepped right up into the chief's face. "You're officially the worst chief of police ever!"

Tenzin placed a hand on Korra's shoulder and pulled her back. "Calm down, Korra. I'll get this sorted out. We just need to be patient."

Korra simmered with rage, but she allowed Tenzin to put an arm around her and guide her toward the exit. They were nearly through the glass front doors when Tenzin turned and called over his shoulder, "But you really are the worst chief. Ever."

Korra had tried to sleep. She'd stared at the ceiling tiles above her bed, willing her eyes to close. She'd even considered trying to meditate, but she couldn't quiet her mind. As a last resort, she'd tried counting koala-sheep. Nothing worked. She couldn't relax when her friends were in jail.

Tenzin had advised her to be patient, but patience had never come easily to her. Tonight was no exception. That was why she'd woken Naga and come all the way to city hall in the middle of the night, why she'd scaled the side of the building, and why she now found herself on the ledge outside Tarrlok's office, peering through a window.

The councilman sat at his desk in the spacious

room, signing documents and handing them over to a council page. Behind him was an enormous stone wall with an intricate dragon seal carved in its center. Water fell in clear sheets down its surface.

From a distance, Tarrlok looked perfectly harmless. Korra knew better. She threw open the window and climbed inside.

"You and I need to talk," she said firmly.

The council page jumped at the unexpected intrusion, but Tarrlok remained calm. He didn't seem at all surprised to see the Avatar. It was almost as if he'd been expecting her.

Tarrlok fixed Korra with a cold stare. He directed his words to the page.

"Are any of the other council members here?" he asked.

"I believe everyone has gone home for the night," the page answered.

"Then you should do the same."

The council page glanced nervously at Korra. The Avatar's mouth was set in a firm line, and her eyebrows slanted downward in an angry scowl. She clearly meant business. "Are you sure, sir?"

"Leave us," Tarrlok commanded.

The page didn't need further convincing. He gathered the signed documents to his chest and slowly backed out of the room. Once the door was shut, Tarrlok spoke.

"You obviously have something on your mind. Spit it out."

"Don't you see? You're doing exactly what Amon says is wrong with benders. You're using your power to impress and intimidate people."

Tarrlok arched an eyebrow. "And you don't?"

"What?" Korra spluttered. "Of . . . of course not."

"Isn't that what you came here to do? Intimidate me into releasing your friends?"

Korra stared at him, speechless.

Tarrlok pushed his chair back from his desk and rose slowly to his feet. "See, that's what I admire about you, Korra, your willingness to go to extremes in order to get what you want. It is a quality we both share."

"You and I are nothing alike!" Korra protested.

"Look, I'll make you a deal." Tarrlok walked slowly around his desk and strolled over to Korra. "You fall in line and do what I say, and I'll release your friends."

The truth hit Korra like a ton of bricks. "That's why you arrested them. To get to me," Korra said. She narrowed her eyes, seething, as she realized the full extent of Tarrlok's cunning.

"I need your answer."

"No." Korra shook her head. "You might be able to

manipulate Chief Saikhan into following you, but it won't work on me."

"You will regret that decision," Tarrlok said darkly.

Korra bristled at his unspoken threat. "You need to be stopped! You're just as bad as Amon."

Tarrlok blinked slowly. When he opened his eyes, something about him had changed. His anger boiled to the surface and a vein throbbed at his temple.

"I've tried to work with you, Korra, but you've made it impossible," he growled. In a flash, Tarrlok whirled away from her toward the water wall behind his desk. He drew a razor-sharp arc of water from the wall and whipped it backward over his shoulder, then forward. The arc lanced out, slicing through the air with a dull whine—headed straight for Korra.

14

With the blade of water flying toward her, Korra gathered her strength and twisted out of the way, her body spiraling through the air like a corkscrew at the last possible moment.

The water blade whistled past just inches from her head, cutting a few strands of hair at the end of her ponytail. Korra landed with a thud on the floor, simultaneously creating a tremor in the ground. The floor split open, churning up jagged fragments of rock that streaked toward Tarrlok as the fissure widened. The rock erupted into the air, punching Tarrlok in the chest and propelling him into the wall of water.

Korra ran forward, blasting Tarrlok with scalding jets of fire. The councilman reared back against the stone wall, leeching water from its surface. He drew the water into a shimmering dome around him, shielding himself from Korra's blasts. Steam rolled off the water dome in curling white puffs as Korra's bursts of flame struck the surface.

Tarrlok touched his fingers to the protective shield of water around him, freezing stray droplets into sharp daggers of ice. From inside the dome, he launched the deadly ice daggers at Korra. The hail of shards flew through the air, the barrage riddling the walls and furniture.

Instinctively, Korra slipped into the complex movements of airbending she had been practicing for months with Tenzin. Even though the wind still did not bend to her command, she danced through the ice daggers, her arms and legs spiraling in complicated patterns. Korra weaved in and out, dodging the ice—even punching some of the shards from the air. But she couldn't avoid them all. Some of the ice daggers nicked her arms and torso, leaving stinging red scratches.

Korra drove her foot into the floor and kicked up a huge slab of marble. The slab rose in front of her like an enormous shield, blocking the razor-sharp shards of ice. Next, Korra reached out with earthbending to the wall behind Tarrlok. With a quick movement of her arms, she heaved the stone wall forward, ramming it into the councilman.

The force of the blow sent Tarrlok reeling. He crashed through the wall of his office onto the balcony above the city council chamber. Momentum carried him over the marble balcony railing. He tumbled through the air but managed to grab the rail with one hand, narrowly avoiding the twenty-five-foot fall to the chamber floor.

Korra ran out onto the balcony to find the councilman dangling precariously.

"Still think I'm a half-baked Avatar?" she taunted.

Tarrlok tried to pull himself up one-handed, but Korra was ready for him. She drove forward with a powerful earthbending strike, causing the marble rail to crumble under his fingers. He fell through the air in a hail of rubble, landing squarely on top of several desks, which broke his fall.

Korra took a running leap off the balcony. She landed on the floor of the council chamber in a deep crouch, punching the ground. The strength of the blow formed a huge crater in the floor, and a rumbling shock wave rippled out from its center. The wave leveled everything in its path, churning up desks, tables, and chairs and tossing them high into the air.

Korra rose to her feet as the wave subsided. She could feel the power coursing through her body. Tarrlok scrambled to back away from her, a look of desperation on his face.

"What are you going to do now? You're all out of

water, pal!" asked Korra. She charged toward Tarrlok, determined to put an end to the battle. Tendrils of flame drifted from her outstretched fingers as she gathered her strength for one final strike.

Suddenly, Korra froze midstep. Her body seized up, unable to move. It was almost as if she'd been turned to stone. The fire at her fingertips dissolved into wisps of smoke. A strange numbness began to spread through her limbs. With growing terror, she recognized the horrible feeling. It was like she'd been chi-blocked, but that was impossible. Tarrlok hadn't even touched her!

Using all her might, Korra dragged her eyes—the only part of her body she was still able to move—upward. What she saw shocked her. The councilman was no longer the smooth, cunning politician who'd tried to cut a deal with her only moments ago. Instead, his eyes were wild. He had the look of a rabid animal.

"You're in my way, Avatar, and you need to be removed," he snarled. Tarrlok's hands were thrust out in front of him. Slowly, he curled his fingers inward, as if jerking a puppet on invisible strings.

Korra gasped as the numbness she felt was replaced by pain. It felt like her skin was crawling, her limbs buckling. In her mind, she struggled against the crippling force that gripped her, but she was helpless to stop it. She was being pushed back, she realized. Her arms and legs were moving against her will. Her body stumbled in a herky-jerky rhythm beyond her control.

"You're . . . you're a Bloodbender?" she croaked.

There were very few Waterbenders with the ability to bloodbend, and even then, bloodbending could only be performed during a full moon, when a Waterbender's strength was at its peak. Bloodbending was a dark and rarely practiced art.

"Very observant," Tarrlok hissed.

"It's not a full moon. How are you doing this?"

"There are a lot of things you don't know about me," he said grimly.

Tarrlok twisted his fingers and Korra's body crumpled to the ground. The blood in her veins had turned against her. Darkness crept in at the edges of her vision. The last thing she saw before the world faded to black was Tarrlok leaning over her.

In the swirling blackness, Korra had a strange vision. It took place in the past. Avatar Aang was there. He was a grown man, and he sat across from the city council members of his day, which included Sokka, his longtime friend. The council sat in judgment on a thin-faced man with a wicked smile. They condemned the man, but he simply chuckled and stretched his clawlike hands out in front of him. Avatar Aang froze midstride, and the rest of the council members went rigid.

The man with the wicked smile was a Bloodbender.

When Korra came to, she found herself tied up in the back of a police transport. Tarrlok stood just outside the vehicle, preparing to slam the rear doors shut.

"Where are you taking me?" Korra demanded.

"Somewhere no one will find you," Tarrlok answered darkly. "Say goodbye to Republic City, Avatar Korra. You'll never see it again."

15

Tenzin could hardly believe his eyes as he rushed into the ruins of the city council chamber. The room was almost completely destroyed. Broken chairs, desks, and tables were strewn about, plaster crumbled from the walls and ceiling, and there was a huge crater in the middle of the floor.

He'd barely been awake when he got the phone call explaining that Avatar Korra was missing and something terrible had happened at city hall. Now, seeing the damage with his own eyes, his anxiety increased tenfold. He ran over to Chief Saikhan, who was standing beside Tarrlok.

"What happened?" Tenzin asked frantically. "What was Korra doing at city hall?"

It was Tarrlok who replied. The councilman looked like he'd been in a fight. He was badly bruised, and his expensive silk robes were torn. He winced as a Waterbender healer tended to the worst of his wounds. "As I told Chief Saikhan, Korra came to my office late last night. She was upset that I arrested her friends. She asked me to release them, and that's when the Equalists attacked."

"This is horrible," Tenzin said.

Tarrlok hung his head. "I tried to protect Korra, but we were outnumbered. Then I was electrocuted."

Tenzin stared at the large burn on Tarrlok's arm. It looked consistent with the type of wound caused by the Equalists' electrified gloves. The Metalbender officers on the scene had already recovered several of them from the rubble.

"When I came to, the police had arrived, but Korra was gone," Tarrlok said. "I'm sorry."

Tenzin nodded, but Tarrlok's apology did little to alleviate his fears. If Korra had been taken to Amon . . .

"Chief Saikhan, mobilize the entire police force. We have to find the Avatar!" Tarrlok commanded.

As Saikhan hurried off to organize the search effort with Tenzin on his heels, Tarrlok smiled to himself. He'd had to move quickly to plant those Equalist weapons in the rubble. He'd even gone so far as to wound himself. Despite the pain, it would all be worth it if he could keep Tenzin and the police from the simple truth. He knew exactly where the Avatar was, and he was determined that no one would find her.

Hospitals were not Lin Beifong's cup of tea. Unfortunately, the injuries she'd sustained during the raid of Hiroshi Sato's secret underground factory were serious enough to land her in one. The former police chief was listening to music from her hospital bed when suddenly a radio announcer's voice cut across the airwaves.

"We interrupt your regularly scheduled broadcast to bring you this special report. Late last night, Equalists attacked city hall, subduing Councilman Tarrlok and capturing Avatar Korra. Details are still coming in, but—"

Beifong switched off the radio and gingerly pushed herself up to a sitting position. She gritted her teeth and climbed to her feet, wincing as she moved her sore body. She walked slowly to the wardrobe across the room and opened its doors to reveal her Metalbender armor. Beifong took a deep breath, steeling herself, and began to suit up.

Her full recovery would have to wait. The Avatar needed her.

In a damp, cold cell deep in the bowels of police headquarters, Asami lay on a cot, staring up at the ceiling. She'd hadn't seen or heard from anyone since she'd been arrested the night before, and she had no idea what had happened to Mako and Bolin.

Korra had promised to send Tenzin to get them out, but it was already noon and there'd been no word. Asami couldn't shake the feeling that something had gone terribly wrong.

She heard footsteps approaching and stood up from her cot just in time to see the metal door of her cell crumple as if it were nothing more than a sheet of paper. Seconds later, the door was jerked free of its hinges. Lin Beifong stood in the empty doorway.

"Hope you got enough beauty rest," said the former chief dryly. "I'm busting you out."

"Thanks. I owe you," Asami replied.

Beifong stepped back into the corridor and motioned for Asami to follow. With her connections in the police department, it hadn't taken her long to find out where Asami, Mako, and Bolin were being held. She walked swiftly through the maze of hallways in the detention block.

Asami knew they'd reached the right cell when she heard familiar voices on the other side of the metal door.

"Are you done yet?" Mako was saying.

"Cover your ears. I can't go with you listening!" Bolin complained.

In one swift movement, Beifong tore the cell door loose to reveal Bolin standing at the toilet in the corner of the room. He glanced over his shoulder, spotted the two women, and squealed in embarrassment. "A little privacy, please!"

Asami ignored Bolin and rushed into Mako's arms, kissing him tenderly.

"Are you all right?" he asked, concerned.

"I'm fine. It's just so good to see you."

"Hate to break up your lovers' reunion, but Korra's in trouble," Beifong interjected. "Amon captured her."

Mako took a step back from her and paled noticeably at the news. "No . . . no, she can't be gone," he said.

"Come on. We have an Avatar to rescue." Beifong waved everyone out of the cell. As Bolin hurried past the ex-chief, he felt the metal zipper in his pants slide closed. His eyes widened in surprise.

"Your fly was down," Beifong said casually.

"Uh, thanks for catching that," Bolin replied, embarrassed.

With Korra in danger, it was clear Team Avatar was needed now more than ever. He couldn't get caught with his pants down.

16

"**S**omebody, help! Please!" Korra shouted.

She'd been calling for help all day, and now her voice was hoarse. She was beginning to think that what Tarrlok had said was true: he'd taken her somewhere no one would ever find her.

Korra beat her hands against the sides of the narrow box closed around her. She felt as if she were in a metal coffin standing on end. The dull thrum of her hands against the metal echoed loudly for a moment, then quickly died.

Defeated, Korra slumped against the side of the box and slid down to her knees. She'd exhausted all her options. The box was utterly unyielding. There was no way out.

Korra shivered as the disjointed memories of Tarrlok bloodbending her into the box came back.

Tarrlok had marched her out of the police transport and forced her into the cellar of an abandoned cabin. There the metal box had been waiting. Tarrlok had maneuvered her inside, his fingers twisted in the air, jerking spasmodically as he controlled her movements like a demented puppet master.

Even now, hours later, she could still feel her skin crawling. *What am I going to do?* Korra thought. *How am I going to get out of here?*

In the darkness, Tenzin's words came back to her: *I urge you to meditate on these visions. I believe Aang's spirit is trying to tell you something.*

Korra settled herself into a cross-legged position and closed her eyes. She'd never liked meditating and wasn't very good at it, but it was worth a shot. She slowed her breathing and turned her focus inward. At first she kept fidgeting, but then her thoughts grew quiet.

Korra emptied her mind, breathing deeply. It wasn't long before a vision began to take shape behind her closed lids.

Toph Beifong marched down the street, flanked by a troop of Metalbender officers. Her shiny black armor clinked as she walked, and the gold badge on her chest gleamed in the afternoon sun. It was the same badge her daughter, Lin, would strip from her own uniform more than forty years later.

Though Toph was blind, she often saw things more accurately than the sighted people around her. An accomplished Earthbender, she could use the earth's vibrations to detect the familiar tread of a dear friend over the footsteps of her officers.

"What are you doing here, Aang? I told you, I have this under control," Toph said.

Avatar Aang stopped in his tracks. He never had been able to sneak up on Toph. "Under normal circumstances, I wouldn't get involved. But if what the victims said is true, we're not dealing with a normal criminal."

Toph placed her hands on her hips. "Fine. Follow me, Twinkle Toes."

"Toph, I'm forty years old." Aang sighed. "You think you could stop with the nicknames?"

Toph shrugged. It didn't matter how old Aang was, or how tall he'd gotten, or what kind of beard he'd grown. On some level, he'd always be that twelve-year-old boy she'd taught to earthbend. "Afraid not," she said.

Toph turned and led her officers into Kwong's Cuisine, one of Republic City's fanciest restaurants. Avatar Aang followed them inside and watched as the police approached a thin-faced man in a corner booth. Two bodyguards stood by while he ate his lunch. As soon as the man spotted Toph, he flashed a wicked smile.

Korra's eyelids fluttered. This man was familiar. She'd seen him before in a vision.

"It's over," Toph said. "You're under arrest, Yakone."

"What is Republic City coming to?" Yakone drawled. "Used to be a man could enjoy his lunch in peace." He turned back to his food, ignoring the chief of police.

Toph lashed out with one of her metal cables and wrapped it around Yakone's wrist. She retracted the cable sharply, jerking him out of the booth.

"What's the big idea?" he complained.

"We have dozens of witnesses, Yakone. We know what you are," Aang said.

Toph released her cable and handed the suspect over to her captain. The officer slapped a pair of metal handcuffs onto Yakone's wrists and marched him toward the door.

"I've beaten every trumped-up charge you yahoos have brought against me, and I'll beat this one too!" he yelled.

Yakone's words echoed in Korra's ears. Her eyes snapped open. She felt slightly dazed, but the feeling quickly wore off as a growing realization dawned on her.

"Whoa! I finally connected with you, Aang," Korra murmured. "But what are you trying to tell me?" She sighed and stared at her surroundings. "A way out of this box would be nice."

Korra closed her eyes again. She had a feeling Aang

wasn't done speaking to her. She was willing to do whatever it took to connect with him again, even if it meant she had to keep meditating.

Tenzin sat behind the desk in his office at city hall. He was on the phone, tracking down leads on Korra's disappearance, when the door flew open and Lin Beifong walked in with Mako, Asami, and Bolin.

The Master Airbender's mouth dropped opened in surprise. He quickly ended his phone call and rose from his desk. "Lin, what are you— You should be in the hospital! And you three—you should be in prison!"

"I figured you could use our help finding Korra," Beifong said.

"You have any leads yet?" Mako asked.

"I've been on the phone all morning, but . . . nothing yet." Tenzin sighed, disappointed.

Mako couldn't stand the thought of waiting around making phone calls while everyone else was out looking for Korra. He was a bundle of nervous energy. He could barely stand still.

"We need Naga. She can track Korra," he told Tenzin.

"I'm afraid her polar bear–dog is missing as well."

"Then where do we start?" asked Bolin.

"My guess is the Equalists are hiding underground, in the maze of tunnels beneath the city," Beifong said.

"Underground. Just like my father's secret factory. Figures." Asami grimaced.

"Yeah, yeah, that makes sense. When those Chiblockers had me in their truck, it sounded like we drove through a tunnel," Bolin added. Recently, he'd been kidnapped by Amon's henchmen. If it hadn't been for Mako and Korra, Amon would have taken his bending away.

Mako considered his brother's words. Suddenly, they sparked a memory.

"I know where to start looking. Come on!" He rushed from the room. Asami and Bolin ran out after him, leaving Tenzin and Beifong to bring up the rear.

"Wherever Amon is keeping Korra, I bet that's where my officers are, too," said the former chief of police.

Tenzin nodded. "Let's bring them all home, Lin."

Tenzin landed Oogi in an abandoned lot on the outskirts of Republic City. He climbed down from the enormous sky bison and helped Beifong, Asami, and

Bolin from the saddle. Mako had already jumped free before the bison had come to a complete stop, and he was running across the empty lot to a narrow alley.

"The truck with Bolin took off down this alley," he said, pointing.

Bolin hurried over to his brother. He looked at the alley closely and then sniffed the air. "This way kinda smells familiar."

Beifong joined the two of them. She metalbent her armored boot apart and slammed her bare foot down on the ground. "There's a tunnel nearby," she confirmed.

The group ran down the alley, which led to a place where the ground sloped under an elevated roadway. At the bottom of the slope, Mako spotted the large, round opening of a sewer tunnel.

"There!" he said.

Beifong studied the ground at the mouth of the tunnel. It was crisscrossed with motorcycle tracks, no doubt created by Amon's Chi-blockers. The ex-chief nodded at Mako. They were on the right path.

17

The sewer tunnels beneath Republic City were a dark, intricate maze of branching pathways and ducts. Mako sparked a flame in his hand and held it aloft to light the way. The group slowly moved forward, on the lookout for any signs of Korra or her Equalist captors. They went straight for as long as they possibly could, and eventually they reached a junction where the path split into three directions.

Mako gritted his teeth. They'd have to make a choice. He plunged forward into the middle tunnel. "Let's try this way."

Asami placed a hand on his arm, stopping him. "And what if Korra's not down there?"

"Then we take another tunnel until we find her!" Mako snapped. He shook free of Asami's hand and struck out down the tunnel. Asami followed him with her eyes, concerned. She let Tenzin and Beifong walk ahead with Mako and fell in beside Bolin.

"Hey, is Mako all right?" she asked. "He seems really worried about Korra."

Bolin shrugged. "Yeah, we all are."

"I know, but . . . he's your brother. Do you think he likes Korra as more than a friend?"

Bolin looked away from her. He scratched the back of his neck nervously. "What? No . . . that's just gossip. Where'd you hear that? Crazy talk is coming out of your mouth right now."

Asami pinned him with an intimidating stare. "What do you know, Bolin? Come on, spill it."

"Nothing! I mean . . . there was this one time during the tournament when Mako and Korra kissed—"

"They kissed?" Asami bit her lip.

"Believe me, I was upset too, but I'm over it." Bolin thought about the crush he used to have on Korra. It felt like ages ago. "I don't think it meant anything."

"I doubt that," Asami said with a hint of anger in her voice. She let her eyes drift to Mako farther down the tunnel. He held his flame high above his head. *Sure, he's lighting the way, but is he also carrying a torch for Korra?* Asami thought.

She was interrupted by the sound of motorcycle engines closing in from behind.

"Hide!" Beifong called.

The group scattered, ducking into small alcoves and slipping into the shadows. Two masked Chi-blockers raced past on motorcycles, their headlights illuminating the tunnel. Beifong watched as one of the Chi-blockers flipped a switch on his motorcycle. A huge stone slab of the tunnel wall rose, revealing a secret passageway. The Chi-blockers rode their bikes into the passage and the wall closed behind them.

After a moment, everyone came out of hiding. Beifong led them over to the hidden door and felt along its surface for the mechanism that would open it. At last, she detected a metal latch on the other side of the wall. She concentrated and metalbent it into position. The wall sprang open and the group hurried inside.

They followed the secret passage until it opened up into what looked like a transportation depot, then quickly ducked into a corner to observe the scene.

Two motorcycles were parked against the far wall of the space, which also housed Equalist tramcars. The metal carts looked like giant sleds that ran on two narrow rails, one in the ground and the other overhead. The trams ran in and out of two tunnels.

A single Chi-blocker stood near the tunnel on the right. Seconds later, he looked up as a tram arrived, carrying more men. The Equalists climbed out of the tram and reported to the Chi-blocker on duty. "Everything's been delivered to the prison, sir."

In their hiding place, Tenzin arched an eyebrow at the others. The prison was nearby, and that tram could take them to it. Beifong nodded, formulating a plan.

After a few minutes, the Chi-blockers walked off, leaving the depot unguarded. The group crept out of hiding and jumped aboard the prison tram, riding it into the dark tunnel.

When the tram pulled out of the tunnel into the prison depot, it was empty. The two Chi-blockers on duty exchanged a puzzled look.

"Must've been a malfunction," one of them said. They turned to the mouth of the tunnel to investigate, when suddenly a flurry of metal cables whipped out of the darkness.

Moments later, Beifong and the others had the Chi-blocker guards bound and gagged.

"You two stay here and keep an eye on them," the former police chief said to Asami and Bolin. They nodded and watched as Beifong stomped the ground again, reading the vibrations in the space around her.

After a moment, she blinked and turned to the group. "My officers are inside."

"What about Korra?" Mako asked desperately.

"I don't see her yet," Beifong said.

Mako looked away from her, disappointed, but there was no time to dwell on his feelings. Beifong took off down the long corridor in front them, eager to find the holding cells.

The former chief used the mental map created by the earth's vibrations to navigate the halls of the Equalist prison. After a few minutes, they came to the end of a winding hallway lined with iron-barred cells. Ahead, two Chi-blocker guards looked up at their approach.

The Chi-blockers reacted immediately, pulling bolas from their belts and spinning the weighted cords over their heads to gather momentum. But before they could release their weapons, Tenzin attacked. He whipped up a furious wind and hurled it at the guards. The hurricane-force blast knocked them into the iron bars of the cells, stunning them.

Mako ran forward and grabbed one of the Chi-blockers by the front of his coat. He dragged the guard to his feet, pushed him up against the wall, and ripped off the man's mask.

"Avatar Korra—where are you keeping her?" Mako yelled heatedly.

Farther down the hall, Beifong located the cell holding the Metalbender officers captured at Hiroshi Sato's underground factory. She metalbent the bars of the cell apart and stepped inside.

The officers looked up when she entered, relieved to see her, but there was a look of unmistakable sadness on their faces.

"I'm too late. That monster already took your bending, didn't he?" Beifong asked.

The officers nodded, confirming her fears.

"I'm so sorry," said Beifong. "Come on. Let's get you out of here."

The former police chief stepped back through the bars and led her men down the corridor. She arrived in time to see Mako brandishing a flame above the palm of his hand and threatening one of the guards.

"I'll ask you one more time. Where is she?"

Frightened, the Chi-blocker cowered. "We don't have the Avatar. And the Equalists didn't attack city hall. Tarrlok's lying."

"What?" Mako asked angrily.

Beifong walked over to Mako and pried the guard's coat from his fingers.

"I scanned the entire prison. She's not here," the ex-chief said to calm the boy.

"Why would Tarrlok make up a story about getting attacked?" said Mako.

Tenzin stepped forward, a look of fury pinching his features as he figured it out. "Because *he* has Korra. He fooled us all!"

Just then, a loud alarm sounded. Startled, the group quickly gathered themselves and raced back to the prison depot.

When they arrived, Asami and Bolin were already waiting on the tram.

"Let's go, people!" Bolin ordered.

Beifong, Tenzin, Mako, and the officers jumped on board and swiftly set the vehicle in motion. The tram glided back into the tunnel, streaking away from the prison. For a moment, it looked as if they might escape undetected, but a second tram barreled into the tunnel behind them, carrying Chi-blockers in pursuit.

Bolin looked out the back of the transport to see Amon's henchmen gaining on them, their faces covered in black cloth and the lenses of their goggles glowing green in the dim light. He lashed out with a powerful earthbending strike, ripping stones from the sides of the tunnel. The walls of the passageway rumbled and caved in behind him. A tumbling mountain of rubble cut off the Chi-blockers and their tram.

"Try to chi-block that, fools!" Bolin gloated.

But there wasn't much time to celebrate. Up ahead, Amon's lieutenant was waiting, kali sticks flaring with electricity. Behind him, an entire troop of Chi-blockers had gathered at the end of the tramline. Two tall mecha-tanks stood by as well, their pincers extended in an unfriendly welcome.

"We've got company!" Beifong shouted, spying the roadblock ahead. "Hold on!"

The ex-chief took aim at the tram rail overhead and tore one end of the iron girder free from its mount. The metal creaked as she bent it down from the tunnel's roof, forming a ramp just a few feet in front of the tram. The speeding metal carriage skipped onto the steep ramp and barreled toward the ceiling. At the last possible second, Beifong tore a hole in the roof of the tunnel, bending rock and debris from the tram's path. The tram smashed through the opening and landed aboveground in a deserted alley, carrying Beifong and the others to safety.

18

Deep in meditation, Korra lost all track of time. There was a part of her that knew she was still trapped inside the narrow metal box at Tarrlok's abandoned cabin, but that part felt very far away. Her immediate thoughts were of the visions playing in her mind. They were memories from her past life as Avatar Aang— something that had happened many years before she was born.

The members of the city council sat around a U-shaped table in the middle of council chambers. There were five members, each representing one of the five kingdoms that made up the United Republic of Nations: the Earth Kingdom, the Fire Nation, the Air Nomads, and the Northern and Southern Water Tribes.

Council Chairman Sokka sat at the center of the table, listening intently as two lawyers argued a case. From his seat in the gallery, Avatar Aang looked at the man on trial.

The thin-faced criminal Yakone sat on a wooden bench beside the council table with his wrists and ankles shackled. He sneered contemptuously at the council members.

"Yakone has ruled Republic City's criminal empire for years," said the prosecuting attorney. "You will hear testimony from dozens of his victims, and they will tell you he has maintained his grip on the underworld by using an ability that has been illegal for decades: bloodbending."

At the sound of the word bloodbending, a murmur rippled through the crowd that had gathered to watch the trial. The prosecuting attorney took a seat, and it was the defense attorney's turn to speak.

"The prosecution's case is built entirely upon the make-believe notion that my client is able to bloodbend at will—at any time, on any day." Yakone's lawyer paused dramatically. "I remind the council that bloodbending is an incredibly rare skill, and it can only be performed during a full moon. Yet the witnesses will claim that my client used bloodbending at every other time except during a full moon. It would be a mockery of justice to convict a man of a crime that is impossible to commit."

Yakone snorted in agreement as his attorney sat down. His trial had only just begun, but he was confident he couldn't be convicted of an impossible crime.

Korra's brow furrowed and sweat beaded on her forehead as the memory flashed forward in time.

After a long deliberation, the council filed into the room and seated themselves around the U-shaped table. A dignified, steely-eyed Sokka stood to announce the verdict.

"In my years, I have encountered people with rare and unique bending abilities. I once bested a man with my trusty boomerang who was able to firebend with his mind. Why, even metalbending was considered impossible for all of history, until our esteemed chief of police, Toph Beifong, single-handedly developed the skill."

Sokka nodded at Toph. The chief stood against the far wall alongside several Metalbender guards.

"The overwhelming amount of testimony and evidence has convinced this council that Yakone is one of these unique benders. And he exploited his ability to commit these heinous crimes," Sokka said. "We find Yakone guilty of all charges and sentence him to life in prison."

Sokka slammed his gavel down on the council table, concluding the trial. Whispers rose throughout the chambers. Yakone's attorney scoffed in disbelief at the ruling, but the criminal himself never even blinked. An eerie smile remained on his lips as he rose slowly from the bench.

Yakone pinned his sharp gaze on the council members and lifted his hands in their heavy metal shackles. His fingers twitched and grasped, clawing the air. Suddenly, the council members seized up, rigid with pain.

Toph Beifong raced toward Yakone, extending the metal cables from her armor. Yakone stopped her with a single twist of his fingers, driving her body backward in a strange, unnatural gait.

Avatar Aang leapt into action, his red and gold Airbender's robes billowing around him. He launched himself at Yakone but lurched to a halt as the Bloodbender speared him with his evil gaze. Aang struggled against the painful grip of Yakone's uncanny ability, calling on the power of the four elements to come to his aid. But all the elements remained silent. The Avatar was helplessly trapped.

Korra's eyes sprang open as the memory abruptly came to an end. She shivered and sagged against the side of the metal box, no closer to finding a way out.

The sun was setting when Oogi touched down on the roof of city hall. The sky bison crouched on his six furry legs and allowed the occupants of his saddle to slide down his wide, flat tail. Tenzin and Beifong dismounted first, followed by Mako, Asami, and Bolin. They'd dropped the rescued Metalbender officers off at police headquarters and headed straight to city hall, looking for Tarrlok.

Tenzin led the others across the roof to a stairwell that took them down into the building. Moments later, they emerged in the council chambers, where Chief Saikhan and three members of the city council stood waiting.

"Thank you all for meeting on such short notice," Tenzin said.

At that moment, Tarrlok walked in with a look of phony concern etched on his features. "Do you have any news of Avatar Korra?" he asked.

"We do," Tenzin answered. He turned to the sly councilman and fixed him with a pointed stare. "*You* kidnapped her."

Chief Saikhan reeled in shock. The other three council members gasped in astonishment.

"I am shocked you would accuse me of such an evil act!" Tarrlok protested. "I already explained—Equalists attacked us and took her."

Mako simmered with rage at Tarrlok's words. He pushed forward, looking to confront the councilman himself, but Tenzin held up a hand to stop him.

"But there were no Chi-blockers here last night," said the Airbender. "You planted the evidence, didn't you?"

Tarrlok backed away from Tenzin nervously. Sweat

broke out on his brow. "That is a ridiculous accusation!"

"It's true! He took her!" a voice shouted.

Everyone turned to see the council page hiding in the corner of the room. He stepped timidly out of the shadows. "I was here when Avatar Korra arrived last night, but Councilman Tarrlok ordered me to leave."

Tarrlok glowered at the page. The fearful little man cowered in response but took a deep breath, steeling himself. "I was on my way out when I saw Tarrlok bring her down to the garage."

"That's nonsense!" Tarrlok said. "Everyone knows you're nothing but a squeaky-voiced liar!"

Beifong studied the page, weighing his words. "Why did you wait until now to fess up?" she asked.

The page gulped in fear. "I was terrified to tell because . . . because Tarrlok is a Bloodbender! He bloodbent Avatar Korra!"

Tarrlok's expression faltered. His smooth politician's mask dissolved.

"Don't make this worse for yourself," Tenzin said firmly. "Tell us where you have Korra."

Tarrlok's eyes grew large. It was clear that he'd been caught. He felt the trap close around him and reacted like a cornered animal.

The councilman lifted his hands, clawing the air

just as Chief Saikhan and Beifong launched their metal cables. The cables never hit their mark. They fell to the ground, limp, as Tarrlok lashed out with his bloodbending. The crushing weight of his power descended on everyone in the room, driving them to their knees. Legs and arms buckled, and bodies writhed in pain as Tarrlok's fingers jerked and twitched. It wasn't long before everyone slumped to the ground, unconscious.

Tarrlok lowered his hands and backed slowly from the council chamber. His days as a politician were over. His days as an outlaw had officially begun.

Avatar Korra consoles her old nemesis Tahno,
another casualty of Amon's war on benders.

Police Chief Beifong uses her earthbending
to locate the Equalists' underground factory.

Korra realizes that Asami
isn't just a prissy rich girl.

At night, Team Avatar goes on
patrol to fight the Equalists.

In the past, Amon's father,
the crime boss Yakone, is put on trial.

Avatar Aang removes the
dangerous Yakone's bending.

Korra bravely braces herself
to escape from Amon's electrified trap.

Amon's forces cast a dark
shadow over Republic City.

As a boy, Amon protected his brother from their cruel father.

Amon claims that Firebenders scarred him when he was a child.

Hurling boulders left and right,
Bolin and Naga come to Asami's rescue.

Korra defiantly delivers a
devastating airbending kick to Amon.

Amon plans a new life with his brother,
but Tarrlok knows it can never be.

The spirit of Avatar Aang appears
and restores Korra's bending.

Korra sees all the Avatars
that have come before her.

With everything set right,
Korra and Mako kiss.

19

Inside the metal box, Korra closed her eyes again. The visions from her past lives were exhausting, but she knew now that they were the key to discovering the truth. She breathed deeply and settled her thoughts. Soon the memory of Yakone's trial surfaced once again.

"You won't get away with this!" Aang shouted. His body was rigid under the Bloodbender's control. He could only watch helplessly as Yakone wrenched his fingers and tightened the grip of his power, pressing Sokka and the other council members until their bodies folded. They struggled against him, but he was too strong. One by one they collapsed, limbs crumpling, and sank into unconsciousness.

Then Yakone whirled and fastened his bloodbending grip on Toph. He guided the police chief's body through the air and forced her to unlock his shackles. Once freed, he tossed her away like a rag doll. She passed out and fell to the ground.

At last, the Bloodbender turned his full attention to Aang, levitating him high into the air. "Republic City is mine, Avatar! I'll be back one day to claim it!"

Suspended in midair, Aang writhed in the grasp of Yakone's bloodbending. Yakone sneered and clenched his fingers. With a simple flick of his wrist, he drew Aang's body across the room and slammed him into the marble floor, knocking him out.

The Bloodbender's lips formed a wicked smile as he turned and fled from the council chambers.

Outside city hall, Yakone jumped into an empty horse cart and took off into the streets of Republic City. He thought he had defeated the Avatar, but as soon as he left the building, Aang's Airbender tattoos started to glow.

The Avatar lay unconscious, but the blue arrow tattoos on the backs of his hands suddenly flared and gave off a blinding light. The tattoo on his head also lit up in a brilliant burst of color. Aang's eyes snapped open. The light faded quickly as he rose to his feet.

Revived, Aang raced out of city hall. He spotted Yakone's cart in the distance, streaking away at breakneck speed. The Avatar summoned a swirling torrent of air beneath his feet. He rode the spiraling current through the streets, zigzagging as he closed in on the escaping carriage.

Yakone glanced over his shoulder and saw Aang rocketing toward him. His eyes widened in disbelief. Before he could even react, the Avatar sliced the cart in two with a razor-sharp blade of air. The horse broke free as the carriage split apart and the halves collapsed, burying Yakone.

Aang was swooping down to pull Yakone from the wreckage when suddenly, the Bloodbender leapt to his feet.

"This time, I'm gonna put you to sleep for good, Avatar!"

Yakone's hands twisted and his fingers gouged the air, snaring Aang in his bloodbending grip. Aang fought the skin-crawling agony as the full force of Yakone's power hammered his body. The Bloodbender was ruthless. He was determined to tear the Avatar apart.

Suddenly, Aang's tattoos flared again, power coursing through his body. It was only for a moment, but it was long enough for him to break free of Yakone's grasp. He drove forward, kicking up slabs of earth. The slabs clapped shut around the Bloodbender, cocooning him in solid rock. Only his head was left exposed.

Aang stood over Yakone. He stared down into the man's wild eyes. "I'm taking your bending away—for good."

Yakone shrank back in terror. "Noooo!" he screamed.

Aang fixed his hands on the Bloodbender's face. Yakone flinched and struggled against him, but the Avatar would not be denied. He pressed a single finger to Yakone's forehead and stripped him of his power.

The Bloodbender's eyes widened. His pupils dilated, then shrank to tiny pinpoints. A blank expression settled over his features, and the scream welling in his throat died on his lips. He shuddered and slipped into unconsciousness.

Avatar Aang dropped his hands and took a step back, exhausted.

"It's over," he whispered wearily.

Korra opened her eyes. She blinked slowly and rubbed a hand across her face, recovering from the intense vision.

"Aang, this whole time you were trying to warn me about Tarrlok," she murmured.

Her thoughts were interrupted by the sound of approaching footsteps. Tarrlok stormed down the cellar stairs and paced angrily in front of the box.

"My life is a disaster now—thanks to you!" he growled.

"So, your little bloodbending secret's out?" Korra asked.

Tarrlok grunted in response.

Korra put her ear to the wall of the metal box,

listening carefully. "And I know how you bloodbent me without a full moon. You're Yakone's son!"

Her words caught Tarrlok off guard. He stopped pacing and stood rooted to the floor.

"I *was* his son, but in order to win Republic City, I had to become someone else." He raked his hands through his hair, agitated. "My father failed because he tried to rule this city from its rotten underbelly. My plan was perfect. I was to be the city's savior. But you— *you* ruined everything!"

"Tarrlok, the jig is up, and you have nowhere to go," Korra said evenly.

"Oh no. I'll escape and start a new life. And you're coming as my hostage." Tarrlok's voice was eerily calm. He turned on his heel and backed away from the box. Korra heard his footsteps retreating as he climbed the cellar stairs.

"You'll never get away with this!" she shouted.

At the top of the stairs, Tarrlok slowed to a dead stop. His eyes darkened as he came face to face with an unexpected visitor.

"Amon!" he said, startled.

The Equalist leader stood in the middle of the cabin, flanked by several Chi-blockers and the Lieutenant. His cruel eyes glinted through the holes in the pale, hard mask that covered his face. He fixed Tarrlok with his deathly stare.

"It is time for you to be equalized," Amon said menacingly.

"You fool! You've never faced bending like mine!" Tarrlok roared.

At once, the Chi-blockers lunged and the Lieutenant whipped his kali sticks from his belt in a shower of sparks. Tarrlok was ready for them. He raised his hands and twisted his fingers in the air, jerking them in a series of complex movements. The Chi-blockers withered, their bodies crumpling under the painful pressure of Tarrlok's bloodbending. They collapsed quickly, dropping to the ground like puppets whose strings had been cut. Even the Lieutenant, a formidable opponent with his electrified fighting sticks, fell in a matter of seconds.

Tarrlok shifted his gaze to Amon. The Equalist leader's eyes were cold and fearless. They bored into Tarrlok. Amon took one step forward and then another. Tarrlok curled his fingers inward by slow degrees, tightening the reins of his bloodbending grasp. Amon's legs stiffened and slowed as if invisible hands were restraining him, but he didn't stop. Incredibly, he kept walking. He advanced with icy determination. With each step, Amon's strength increased, until the stiffness left him. He brushed off Tarrlok's bloodbending as easily as he might swat a bumble-fly.

Tarrlok stared in utter disbelief. "Wh-wh-what are you?"

"I am the solution," Amon answered. In a flash, he grabbed Tarrlok's wrists in his hands and drove him to his knees. The instant Amon touched him, his bloodbending grip on the Lieutenant and the other Chi-blockers was broken.

Tarrlok gasped in terror. He struggled as Amon leaned over him and clutched his face in his clawlike hands. It was no secret that the Equalist leader could strip people of their bending powers, and Tarrlok knew that he was about to become Amon's next victim. A piercing scream rose on his lips but died the instant Amon touched a finger to his forehead. One last burst of energy spiked through him before it winked out, extinguished forever. Unconscious, Tarrlok slumped to the ground.

20

Korra heard Tarrlok's scream from her prison inside the metal box. It was a chilling sound, but what she heard next was even more terrifying.

"I'll take care of him," Amon said. "You four retrieve the Avatar. Do not underestimate her. Electrocute the box to knock her out before you open it."

Korra froze at the sound of footsteps tramping down the cellar stairs. She looked desperately at the inside of the box. There was no escape. The walls were solid metal. The only part of the box that wasn't solid was the very top, which was crisscrossed by a grate of metal bars. The small, square holes allowed air to circulate, but they weren't large enough for a person to squeeze through.

Just then, Korra had an idea. She pulled off one of her leather armbands and tore it, creating a narrow strip of fabric. She looped the fabric over one of the bars in the grate and grasped the ends tightly, one in each hand. As the footsteps drew closer to the box, Korra hung from the fabric, tucking in her legs and elbows so that no part of her touched the metal.

Outside the box, the Lieutenant moved into position. His kali sticks rippled with electricity. He thrust them against the front of the box and watched as the current crackled over the surface. He heard the Avatar scream inside, but he wasn't about to stop. She was an impressive opponent. He had to make sure she was knocked out.

After a few more moments, the Lieutenant withdrew his kali sticks and returned them to his belt. He listened carefully and was satisfied when he heard a body drop to the floor.

The Lieutenant ordered the Chi-blockers to open the box and was pleased when he saw the Avatar lying in a crumpled heap at the bottom. He signaled to the Chi-blockers to tie her up.

The Chi-blockers were moving in, drawing bola cords from their belts, when Korra jumped to her feet and kicked out with a huge burst of fire. Startled, the Equalists reared back, their masks singed by the billowing cloud of flame.

Korra leapt from the box and slammed her fist down on the cellar floor, stirring up an undulating wave of rock. Jagged stones flew from the floor, ramming into the Equalists. Korra raced past them and flew up the cellar steps two at a time.

Outside the cabin, nestled on the slope of a snowy mountain, Amon was loading Tarrlok's unconscious body into a waiting cargo truck. He closed the vehicle's doors and turned back to the cabin just in time to see Korra stumble out into the snow. She looked around wildly, completely unfamiliar with her surroundings, and then she saw Amon—a dark, familiar threat against the snowy landscape.

Amon's eyes met hers and narrowed in rage. He took a step toward her, but Korra was quick to react. She drew a crumbling sheet of snow from the ground and bent its powdery surface into pointy spikes of ice. She whipped the spikes out in front of her, directly into Amon's path. The shards didn't stop him, but they were enough to buy her time. Panicked, she kicked up a screen of snow, temporarily blinding Amon as she disappeared down the steep slope of the mountain.

Seconds later, the Lieutenant and Chi-blockers emerged from the cabin. They began to pursue the Avatar, but Amon shook his head and gestured for them to wait. There would be plenty of time to deal with Korra later. He would see to it personally.

Her heart pounding, Korra slid down the side of the mountain. She glided across the surface of the snow, weaving between rocks and trees. She was sliding fast, rapidly gaining momentum, until her foot caught on a rock and she went tumbling hard into the trunk of a tree. The impact knocked the wind out of her, but she knew she had to keep moving.

Korra struggled to push herself up from the ground, but her arms gave way and she collapsed back into the cold snow. Her eyes fluttered closed.

Korra woke to something soft and wet lapping her face. Slowly, she opened her eyes to see her polar bear–dog, Naga, hovering over her.

"Naga, you came looking for me. Good girl," Korra said groggily.

Naga thumped her tail in excitement. The polar bear–dog had been tracking Korra's scent ever since she'd disappeared from city hall.

Korra tried to get up, but she was still too weak to stand. Naga helped her master up onto her back, where she collapsed across the saddle. Luckily, Naga knew the way.

The polar bear–dog turned and bounded through the snow, heading back toward Republic City.

Fortunately, it hadn't taken Tenzin and the others long to recover from Tarrlok's bloodbending attack in city council chambers. As soon as they'd come to, they'd wasted no time following Tarrlok's trail. Chief Saikhan alerted the Metalbender police, while Tenzin, Beifong, Mako, Asami, and Bolin used Oogi the sky bison to search for Korra from the air.

They'd been flying over Republic City for hours. Everyone was on the verge of losing hope when Mako spotted Naga galloping through the narrow streets near the docks. Korra was draped across her saddle.

Tenzin immediately brought Oogi down to land near the polar bear–dog.

"Korra! Thank goodness!" he said. He climbed down from Oogi's saddle, and the others quickly followed him. Everyone rushed toward Korra, eager to see if she was okay. They closed in around Naga. Korra smiled up at them weakly.

"Where's Tarrlok?" Beifong asked. "How did you get away?"

Mako pushed past the former police chief. "Give her some space," he said. Ignoring the others, he pulled Korra gently from Naga's saddle and scooped her up in his arms. He walked away from everyone else, cradling Korra against his chest.

"I was so worried," he said softly. "Are you all right?"

Korra could barely keep her eyes open. All she knew was that she felt safe and warm in Mako's arms. "I'm fine," she whispered. "I'm so glad you're here."

Korra settled herself against Mako's chest and drifted off to sleep. Mako sighed and rested his chin on top of her head. He walked up Oogi's wide, flat tail into the sky bison's saddle and set Korra down tenderly.

"You're safe now," he said.

Silently, Asami watched, crushed, as Mako brushed several loose strands of hair from Korra's face.

21

Air Temple Island was peaceful and quiet when the sun came up over the horizon. The night before had been filled with the hustle and bustle of Tenzin's return with the newly rescued Avatar, but this morning, a sense of calm prevailed.

Korra slept soundly on a cot in the family common room. Though Jinora, Ikki, and Meelo were eager to see her, Tenzin kept them at bay. After all she had been through, the Avatar needed to rest.

Mako kept watch by Korra's bedside. He clasped her hand in his as she slept. Asami looked on from the doorway, struggling with her hurt feelings. She was as happy as anyone to have Korra back, but she wasn't happy about the way Mako was acting.

By midafternoon, Korra was back on her feet. She woke up starving and headed straight for the family dining table.

"The food tastes amazing, Pema," Korra said after finishing her third bowl of noodles. "I'm finally starting to feel like myself again."

Pema, Tenzin's very pregnant wife, looked at Korra and smiled. "We're so thankful you're home safe." She rose and began to collect the dishes from the table. Asami, who was seated across from Korra and next to Mako, offered to help, and the two women walked off to the kitchen.

Tenzin leaned forward where he sat between Beifong and Bolin. He spoke gently to Korra. "I realize you've been through a lot, but I need to know everything that happened."

Korra nodded and took a deep breath. "Well, first off, Tarrlok isn't who he says he is. He's Yakone's son."

Tenzin and Beifong exchanged looks.

"It all makes sense now," the ex-chief said. "That's how Tarrlok was able to bloodbend us without a full moon."

"But how did you escape? And where's Tarrlok?" Tenzin asked.

"Amon captured him and took his bending."

"What?" Tenzin's eyes widened in shock.

"Yeah, he showed up out of nowhere. He almost got me, too." Korra shivered a little and wrapped her arms around herself.

"This is very disturbing news," Tenzin said. "Amon is becoming emboldened. Taking out a councilman, almost capturing the Avatar. I fear Amon is entering his endgame."

An uncomfortable silence settled over the room.

In the kitchen, Asami placed an armload of dishes into the sink. Pema turned on the water and began to wash them. A couple of minutes later, Pema cried out, placing a hand on her belly.

"Pema, are you all right?" Asami asked.

Tenzin's wife straightened and took a deep breath. "I'm fine. The baby is just . . . kicking really hard."

Asami's features were etched with concern.

"Should I get Tenzin?" she asked.

"No reason to worry him." Pema sighed. "It's nothing."

At that moment, Mako walked into the room, holding an empty teapot. "Can I get some more hot water? Korra needs more tea."

Asami didn't budge. She folded her arms across her chest. "You're a Firebender. Boil it yourself."

Pema glanced up and sensed the tension between the two of them. "I'm going to step out, in case you two want to talk," she said. She dried her hands on a dish towel and quietly left the kitchen.

Mako looked after her, puzzled. "Is there something we need to talk about?" he asked Asami.

Asami stared hard at him. At last, she spoke.

"I've noticed how you treat Korra. How you acted when she was missing. You have feelings for her, don't you?"

"What? No!" Mako replied, flustered. "She was taken by a crazy Bloodbender! How did you expect me to act?"

"I like Korra, but you've been keeping the truth from me this whole time!"

"The truth? About what?"

Asami sighed deeply. "You're really going to make me say it?"

"Yes, because I don't know what you're talking about!" Mako said, exasperated.

"The kiss, Mako. I know."

"I . . . well . . ." Mako's voice trailed off. He flushed a brilliant shade of red from the base of his neck all the way up to his hairline. It was true. He had kissed Korra—or rather, Korra had kissed him. They'd been arguing about her going out with Bolin. She'd accused him of being jealous, he'd denied it, and all of a sudden she'd kissed him and left him thoroughly confused.

His feelings were always confused as far as Korra was concerned.

Mako blinked, suddenly angry. "Bolin told you, didn't he?"

"Don't blame your brother for what you did. Do you have feelings for Korra or not?" Asami asked insistently.

Mako looked at Asami and softened. He reached out and put a hand on her shoulder. "Look, things are crazy right now. Can we deal with our relationship problems later?"

"There might not be any relationship to worry about later," Asami said coldly. She shrugged off his touch and stalked out of the kitchen.

Mako groaned and covered his face with his hands.

Outside the family living quarters on Air Temple Island, Tenzin pulled Beifong aside.

"Lin, I need to ask you a favor." Tenzin wrung his hands nervously as he rambled. "It would mean the world to me, but I know it could be a potentially awkward situation. Furthermore—"

"Spit it out already!" she said.

"Will you stay here and watch over Pema and the

children while I meet with the council? With everything that's happened lately, I want to be sure my family is in safe hands."

Tenzin glanced at Beifong, trying to gauge her reaction. The two of them had a history together. In fact, they'd been in a serious relationship before Pema had confessed her feelings to Tenzin years ago. Korra had jokingly accused Tenzin of breaking Beifong's heart, but it was clear now, as the ex-chief placed a hand on Tenzin's shoulder, that there were no hard feelings.

"Of course I'll help, old friend."

Tenzin smiled, relieved, and thanked her.

Just then, Pema walked out of the house holding Meelo in her arms. She frowned when she noticed Beifong's hand on her husband's shoulder.

"I didn't realize you two were out here," she said sharply.

"Pema! Yes. Lin has agreed to help out around here and keep an eye on things while I'm away."

Pema glanced at Beifong. "Thank you," she said. "I could use the extra pair of hands." She walked over to the former police chief and deposited Meelo into her arms. "Would you mind giving him a bath? He's filthy."

Meelo grinned and squirmed in Beifong's arms, pawing her coat with grimy fingers. Pema turned and walked back inside the house, while Tenzin strode out into the courtyard, calling for Oogi.

"This is not what I signed on for!" Beifong called after him.

Tenzin simply waved and climbed up into his sky bison's saddle.

Meelo giggled and said, "I gotta poo! Real bad!"

Beifong extended one of her metal cables and wrapped it around the four-year-old's waist, dangling him at arm's length. She wrinkled her nose in disgust and carried him into the house.

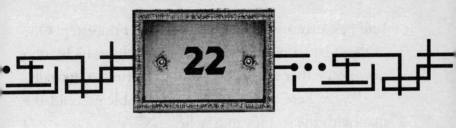

22

The Fire Nation councilwoman could often be disorganized, but today it seemed as if she had managed to do a thousand little things wrong. She had even misplaced her house keys before she left for work. Her husband watched with concern as she searched their home from one end to the other, turning out pockets and opening drawers.

Being a councilwoman was no easy job, and her husband supposed that with everything that had happened lately, his wife was under additional stress. There were only four council members left since Tarrlok was revealed to be a Bloodbender, and with the threat of Amon and his Equalist revolution, they all had their hands full.

The councilwoman found her keys at last and kissed her husband goodbye. She was just about to leave when a knock sounded at the front door. She opened it to find two exterminators standing on her doorstep. One of them had a peculiar-looking mustache, which hung down on either side of his mouth like fire ferrets' tails.

"We're here to fix a spider-rat problem," said the man with the strange mustache.

"I didn't call an exterminator," the councilwoman responded, confused.

In a flash, Amon's lieutenant pulled his kali sticks from inside his exterminator's uniform, the tails of his mustache wagging as he electrocuted the councilwoman. She passed out and toppled over into his arms.

Tenzin landed Oogi on the roof of city hall and quickly dismounted. He was eager to begin the day's council session with the remaining members in the hopes that they could find a way to defeat Amon. He walked swiftly across the roof, headed for the stairs. Suddenly, he got the strange feeling he was being watched.

Tenzin looked around. Everything on the roof seemed perfectly normal. Three window washers hung from the round dome of one of the building's towers, cleaning the clear glass panels. Tenzin shook off the feeling and kept walking.

He had almost reached the stairwell when the air shifted around him. A current of static electricity rippled through his beard, causing the hairs to stand on end. Tenzin whirled just in time to see three electrified bola disks hurtling toward him. He flipped out of the way, dodging the disks and their sparking cords. When he looked to see where they had come from, he noticed the window washers closing in on him. They were Equalists in disguise.

Tenzin pivoted sharply and flung a powerful blast of air at his attackers. The Equalists scattered, the ferocious wind driving them to fan out across the rooftop. They regrouped swiftly, however, and launched several bolas. One of the bolas whirled past Tenzin's head, completely missing its target, but the other two were direct hits. They tangled around his wrists.

Amon's henchmen jerked the bola cords, wrenching Tenzin's arms out in front of him. While two of the men held him steady, the third leapt into the air with a spinning kick aimed straight for Tenzin's head. The Master Airbender dodged the attack as best he could with his arms restrained. He arched backward, narrowly avoiding the kick. The Equalist sailed past just a hairsbreadth from Tenzin's face, landing a few feet behind him.

Outnumbered and at a clear disadvantage, Tenzin

summoned the power of the wind to even the score. The air stirred and spiraled toward him. Currents swirled and swept through his robes, rustling the fabric. Tenzin began to spin, drawing the air into a whirling vortex beneath his feet. The Equalist behind him was sucked in and spit back out, slamming into the stone wall around the edge of the roof.

The vortex rose higher and higher, gathering strength and momentum and propelling Tenzin upward on a funnel of air. The Equalists attached to his wrists were caught up in the churning cyclone. After several dizzying rotations, they couldn't hold on to the bola cords any longer. Their fingers slipped loose and they were flung far out into the sky. Tenzin watched as the Equalists receded into the distance. He had no idea where they would land.

With his enemies overcome, he allowed the funnel of air to dissolve and landed gently on the roof. As soon as his feet touched the ground, the council page rushed out of the stairwell to meet him.

"I'm so relieved to see you!" the page squeaked.

"The other council members—are they all right?" asked Tenzin.

"I'm afraid not. I've just received a call from Chief Saikhan. They've all been captured!"

Tenzin shook his head, stunned. "This can't be happening."

"The leadership of Republic City is in your hands now, sir," the page said somberly.

Just then, they heard a loud explosion in the distance. Tenzin and the council page ran to the edge of the roof and looked out over the wall. Dark, billowing smoke rose into the sky. There was a building on fire a few blocks away. Before Tenzin could even react, a series of dull booms followed as a coordinated chain of explosions rocked the city. Plumes of smoke drifted into the air, and on the horizon, a fleet of Equalist airships crept into view.

"This is a tragic day indeed!" the page said sadly.

Tenzin nodded in sorrow. There was no turning back now. Republic City was under attack.

High above the city streets in an Equalist airship, Hiroshi Sato held a small gold locket in his palm. He stared at the photograph inside. It was a family portrait of him with his late wife and his daughter, Asami. It had been taken many years ago, when Asami was still a little girl.

It was the family Hiroshi had always wanted, but benders had taken it all away. Hiroshi sighed and closed the locket, tucking it into his jacket pocket. He walked over to Amon, who stood at the windows, looking out at the attack under way.

"I've dreamed of this day for so long," Hiroshi said.

"Yes," Amon answered. His voice was full of menace. "The time has come for the Equalists to claim Republic City as their own."

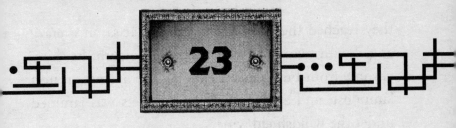

23

Team Avatar wasn't about to stand by while Amon waged his war on Republic City. Korra, Mako, Asami, and Bolin saw the explosions from the shores of Air Temple Island and immediately sprang into action.

They took a boat across the bay and landed at the city's docks. Police sirens wailed as Metalbender officers crisscrossed the town, helping people escape ruined buildings and confronting the invading Equalist forces.

In the midst of the confusion, Asami scanned the narrow grid of streets leading away from the docks and turned to Korra. "Where'd you say you parked the car?"

"It's right around here somewhere," the Avatar answered. She peered down several side streets until she saw what she was looking for. "There it is!"

Korra pointed out the sleek black hot rod. It was parked midway down a busy road lined with shops. Team Avatar hurried over. Asami's eyebrows rose once they reached the sporty Sato-mobile. It sat at a crazy angle, with two of its wheels up on the curb. Its shiny chrome front bumper was rammed up against an iron lamppost, and a slew of parking tickets was jammed under the windshield wipers.

"Wow. Nice parking job," Asami said sarcastically.

"Hey, you guys got arrested and left me alone with the car. I made it very clear I don't know how to drive." Korra put her hands on her hips, defensive.

"All things considered, you did a great job. But how are we going to pay all these parking tickets?" Bolin asked.

Mako leaned over and snatched the tickets from the windshield. He clapped them together between his hands and incinerated them with a burst of flame. Bolin gasped at his older brother's blatant disregard for the law.

"Relax," Mako said. "The city is under attack. The police have more important things to worry about."

While Bolin mulled over his brother's actions, Asami pulled her Equalist glove from the trunk of the car and slipped it on. She took her position in the driver's seat and waited for the rest of the team to climb in.

Mako opened the passenger-side door and moved to slide in beside Asami, but her chilly words stopped him. "Why don't you sit in back. With Korra."

"I think I will," he grumbled, slamming the door in a huff.

Mako hopped into the backseat next to Korra.

"Everything all right?" she asked.

"Yeah, everything's terrific," he muttered.

Korra could tell from his prickly tone and the way Asami peeled out into the road, tires squealing, that everything was far from all right.

The command center in police headquarters was a flurry of activity. Chief Saikhan stood behind a bank of dispatchers, clerks, and Metalbender officers operating a huge telephone switchboard. Reports poured in from all over the city with news of the Equalist attack.

"Chief, Air Unit Seven was just taken out by an Equalist airship!" a dispatcher announced.

"Send a River Rescue unit!" Saikhan barked.

A second clerk spoke up, repeating information streaming in through her headset. "Chief, all the River Rescue ships have been sabotaged!"

"What?" Saikhan scrubbed a hand over his face, clearly overwhelmed. He looked up to see Tenzin striding purposefully into the command center.

"Am I glad to see you," the chief said. "I was afraid you'd been captured, too!"

"I'm the only council member left. What's the status?" Tenzin asked.

"Amon has launched simultaneous attacks across the boroughs. The police are trying to regain control, but we're spread too thin."

Tenzin weighed Saikhan's words, trying to decide the best course of action. After several moments of frowning and stroking his close-cropped beard, he came to a decision. "I need to send a wire."

"To whom, Councilman?" asked an eager clerk.

"To the general of the United Forces."

The United Forces was the military arm of the United Republic of Nations. It was made up of soldiers and benders from the Water Tribes, the Earth Kingdom, and the Fire Nation and had been formed to protect citizens in the event of danger. Tenzin knew the time had come to call on them.

One of the dispatchers rapidly tapped out Tenzin's message on a telegraph machine. "Councilman, your message has been sent!"

Tenzin barely had time to thank the clerk before the power failed and the lights in the command center blinked off. At the same moment, the phone lines went dead. The police clerks gasped, but soon a shaft of light sliced through the darkness. Chief Saikhan held up a flashlight. He tossed a second flashlight to Tenzin, who quickly switched it on.

Just then, everyone heard a loud hissing noise. Tenzin aimed his flashlight into the corners of the room to investigate and spotted a cloud of white gas flooding into the command center through the metal air vents overhead.

Saikhan reacted quickly, slamming the vents closed with metalbending, but the gas continued to seep into the room underneath the door.

"We need to evacuate!" Tenzin said urgently. "Everyone stay close to me!"

He pushed open the door to the command center. It opened onto a dark, gas-filled corridor. Thinking fast, Tenzin created a giant bubble of clean air and enveloped Chief Saikhan and the others in its protective cocoon as he guided them slowly down the hall toward the exit.

When they finally emerged into the courtyard outside, Tenzin let the bubble dissolve. No sooner had he lowered his defenses than he noticed they were surrounded. A line of Hiroshi Sato's mecha-tanks formed a ring around the courtyard, closing them in.

"Not these mecha-tanks again!" Tenzin groaned.

The tanks raised their arms, lifting the heavy metal pincers Tenzin remembered—only this time, the arms looked different. Instead of two grasping claws, each machine had only one. The second claw had been replaced with a powerful electromagnet. Chief Saikhan and his officers looked up in alarm. Their metal armor made them easy targets.

The mecha-tanks leveled their arms at the Metalbenders. With a high-pitched whine, the electromagnets flared to life, dragging the officers forward. Unable to withstand the magnetic current, the police flew through the air until they collided with the flat, hard surface of the magnets.

Chief Saikhan was the last of the Metalbenders caught in the powerful pull. As he tumbled through the air, Tenzin mounted a counterattack. He lassoed the chief with a strong current of air, trying to wrestle him away from the tanks. Saikhan hung suspended in midair for a moment, but the magnet was too strong. Tenzin lost his hold on the chief, and he was sucked into the enemy's clutches.

Three of the tanks pulled away to load the officers into a nearby prisoner transport, but the remaining three rolled toward Tenzin on heavy rubber treads. They launched grappling hooks at the end of long cables, hoping to trap him in their two-pronged grasp. Tenzin skillfully evaded the hooks and lashed out with quick airbending strikes. He whipped the hooks off course with concentrated blasts of air, deflecting them from the police clerks still sheltering behind him.

A mecha-tank rumbled forward, driving its heavy platinum claw directly at Tenzin. He flipped backward to avoid it, but at the same time, a second tank lashed out with a grappling hook. The hook slammed into Tenzin and drove him into the hard stone wall of police headquarters.

Tenzin reeled from the impact. Dazed, he stumbled away from the wall and dropped to his knees as a wave of fatigue rushed over him. Blackness seeped in around the edges of his vision. His eyes began to close. As he drifted toward unconsciousness, what he saw troubled him. The prisoner transport sped off, carrying Chief Saikhan and the Metalbenders to Amon. A police airship plummeted from the sky, black smoke leaking from its damaged gondola. A cargo truck arrived and Chi-blockers leapt out, capturing the police clerks.

Tenzin struggled to remain conscious, but it was no use. He passed out, his last thought the terrible certainty that the tides had turned in favor of Amon.

24

As Tenzin sank into unconsciousness, a black hot rod rounded the corner and sped toward the courtyard in front of police headquarters.

With a loud rumble, an earth ramp sprang up from the ground. The hot rod drove straight onto the ramp and launched off the end. As the car sailed through the air, Korra, Mako, Asami, and Bolin jumped out. Team Avatar had arrived!

The Sato-mobile continued on its course, crashing into a mecha-tank in a blaze of fire and smoke. The tank fell over backward and hit the ground with an earsplitting clang.

Team Avatar struck out across the courtyard. Mako raced forward and unleashed a barrage of fire bursts at the other tanks. The flames whistled through the air and bounced off the platinum-plated machines.

Bolin fell in beside his brother, stomping the ground and kicking up chunks of rock. He flung more rocks at the tanks, pelting them mercilessly. Still the tanks rumbled forward, crushing the rocks beneath their treads.

One of the tanks raised its claw arm with a hydraulic hiss. It hurled a grappling hook directly at Mako. The hook shot out across the courtyard and clamped shut, trapping the Firebender. Mako struggled in the grip of the grasping talon. His eyes widened as electricity crackled along the cable connected to the hook. In an instant, the current arced through his body. He gasped in pain.

Mako grimaced, fighting the strength of the electrical shock. He fastened his hands around the cable and summoned lightning between his palms, then forced the lightning along the cable, reversing the current. Sparks flew as the electricity rippled back toward the tank. The mecha-tank shuddered, and its lights dimmed as it shorted out.

A few feet away, Korra rushed toward an oncoming tank, trailing jets of water from her fingers. She ran up the earth ramp and somersaulted high into the air above the machine. When she was directly over the tank, she forced the water down two of its exhaust pipes. The engine sputtered and the tank slowed to a stop. Steam hissed from its vents. Bolin knelt and punched the earth, churning up rock beneath the rubber treads. The mecha-tank toppled over and hit the ground with a thud.

In the middle of the battle, Asami caught sight of Tenzin. He was unconscious, and two Chi-blockers were loading him into a cargo truck. Asami sprinted toward the truck, coming up behind the two Chi-blockers. She grabbed the first and zapped him with her Equalist glove. As his body slumped to the ground, the second Chi-blocker charged her with a series of precise strikes. She dodged the strikes and landed a few swift punches before she finally zapped him.

At that moment, Tenzin came to in the back of the truck. He saw Asami and her friends and let out a sigh of relief. The Master Airbender climbed to his feet and jumped back into the fight, blasting a mecha-tank sky-high with a fierce gust of air. He stood firm beside Team Avatar, driving back the Equalist attack, while the whine of an airship's engines buzzed overhead.

On board the Equalist airship hovering above police headquarters, Hiroshi Sato peered down through a telescope. He watched in distress as his daughter and her friends defeated his mecha-tanks.

"Tenzin has escaped once again," he said to Amon. "I can't stand to see Asami fighting alongside those benders."

The Equalist leader remained calm. His eyes were cold and unblinking behind his mask. This was just one small part of his elaborate plan. There would be plenty of opportunity to bring the Avatar and her friends to heel.

"We will capture them before long," Amon said evenly, "and you will have your daughter back."

The courtyard was littered with the twisted metal shells of broken mecha-tanks and the bodies of unconscious Chi-blockers. Korra picked her way through the debris and rushed over to Tenzin. "Are you all right?" she asked, worried.

"I'm fine," Tenzin answered. "Thank you, kids. Another moment later and I would have been on my way to Amon."

Just then, Mako interrupted with unwelcome news. "Uh, guys . . . look," he said, pointing. Everyone turned to see an Equalist airship in the distance. It loomed over the bay, headed straight for Air Temple Island.

Tenzin and Korra stared in horror. Amon had brought the fight to their home.

25

The shadow of the Equalist airship fell across the shores of Air Temple Island like an angry black cloud. Air Acolytes hurried into the Air Temple tower, and the White Lotus sentries, a special order of warriors charged with training and protecting the Avatar, raced from their barracks toward the island's main gate.

Lin Beifong stood outside the family's living quarters near the center of the island. From her vantage point, she could see the airship in the distance, hovering above the shoreline. She watched with a mounting sense of unease as the ship's cargo bay dropped open and a thick cable shot out from inside. The cable smashed into the ground, lodging firmly in the outcrop of the island's rocky beach. Seconds later, Chi-blockers latched on to the cable and slid down its length to land on the shore.

Pema and her children stood behind Beifong,

huddled in the doorway of their home. They gasped in fear as the Equalists launched their invasion.

"Everyone hide inside and remain calm," Beifong ordered.

Pema wailed, doubling over in pain.

"Pull it together, Pema!" Beifong scolded. "Didn't I just say to remain calm?"

Pema clutched her pregnant belly and took a deep breath. The Equalists weren't the only ones who wanted to join them on Air Temple Island.

"Mommy, what's wrong?" Ikki asked, frightened.

"The baby's coming," Pema moaned.

"Oh no!" Jinora said.

"Not now, baby!" Meelo cried.

"Think you could've picked a better time to come into this world, child," Pema murmured to her unborn baby. "I love you, but really!"

An elderly Air Acolyte woman appeared in the doorway. She wrapped a comforting arm around Pema's shoulders and led her and the children inside.

At the beach, a second airship arrived and hovered next to the first. Within moments, another cable struck the ground and more Chi-blockers slid down to the rocky shore. Amon's lieutenant sped down the zip line. As soon as his feet touched the ground, he pulled his electrified kali sticks from his belt, ready for battle.

The Lieutenant led the first charge of Chi-blockers up the steep stone steps that led to the island's main gate. A line of White Lotus sentries stood at the top of the steps, determined to drive back the Equalists. They rained fire, water, and earth down on the heads of their attackers.

The Chi-blockers drew their bolas as they rushed the stairs, twirling the weapons over their heads. In unison, they launched the bolas. The cords sliced through the air, colliding with the onslaught of flame, water, and rock. The resulting clash echoed across the island.

The sound reached Beifong in front of the family's house. She knew it was only a matter of time before the battle came to her. The White Lotus sentries were skilled warriors, but they were clearly outnumbered.

The former police chief hunkered down to wait.

The elderly Air Acolyte reached out and grasped Pema's hand. She had made Tenzin's wife as comfortable as possible in the bedroom at the back of the house, farthest from the noise of the fighting. This was not an ideal time to have a baby, but neither she nor Pema had a choice in the matter.

Pema was propped up in bed. Her face was covered in sweat. Her hair was damp and clung to her forehead. She was in labor, and the baby was coming fast.

She looked wildly around the room, alarmed to discover that her children were nowhere in sight.

"The children—where are they?" Pema asked.

"Don't worry," the Air Acolyte said soothingly. "They're in the other room, totally safe."

Pema nodded, but she wasn't reassured. The sound of the fighting was drifting closer. She'd rather have her children where she could see them.

Beifong saw the pale green glint of the Lieutenant's goggles before she spotted the rest of him. He emerged over the crest of a hill, leading several masked Chi-blockers straight for her. The Chi-blockers fanned out in front of him, twirling bolas.

Beifong broke from her position in front of the house, meeting her opponents at a dead run. She extended two of the metal cables from her armor. They snaked out like mechanical tentacles, spiraling through the air to close around two of the Equalists. Beifong jerked her cables roughly, knocking the two Chi-blockers together in a satisfying crunch of flesh and bone.

She tossed the unconscious Equalists aside and retracted her cables before rounding on the three men racing toward her. Beifong whirled and kicked up pillars of jagged rock from the ground. One of the pillars smashed into a Chi-blocker and sent him flying into the side of the house.

Beifong rammed her foot into another pillar, kicking off massive hunks of rock. The rock plowed into two oncoming Equalists and smashed them in the stomach. Winded and bruised, they dropped to the ground.

The Lieutenant stepped forward, impatient to stop Beifong. Sparks leaked from the tips of his kali sticks, and he swirled them in a complex pattern of movements. The former police chief wasn't one to be distracted by a few sparks. She launched her metal cables and looped them around the Lieutenant's wrists.

Despite his dire circumstances, the Lieutenant grinned. In a flash, he touched his kali sticks to Beifong's cables. Electricity sparked and raced down the metal wire, electrocuting Beifong.

The ex-chief moaned in pain and dropped to her knees. When she looked up, the Lieutenant was standing over her, sparking rods poised to deliver his final blow.

"Stay away from my Dad's ex-girlfriend!" a voice shouted.

Beifong shifted her gaze to see Tenzin's older daughter swoop down from above on her air glider. Jinora landed behind the Lieutenant and collapsed the wooden wings of her glider into a fighting staff. She used the staff to channel a powerful blast of air that sent the Lieutenant flying across the courtyard.

Beifong climbed to her feet. "Jinora, you shouldn't be out here!"

Just then, Ikki sped out from behind the house, riding on a spinning globe of air. She zigzagged across the courtyard, bowling into Chi-blockers left and right. "Get off our island!" she yelled.

"Girls, you need to go back inside this instant!" Beifong cautioned.

Not only did Tenzin's children refuse to retreat, but their ranks grew. Meelo hopped out of the house with a fierce battle cry.

"Taste my fury!" he screamed.

"No, Meelo!" Beifong said.

The four-year-old hurled himself at the Chi-blockers, farting wild blasts of air into their faces. Meelo's blasts were as powerful as they were stinky. He sent the remaining Equalists crashing into the side of the house. They staggered and dropped to the ground, unconscious.

"Never mind," Beifong muttered, looking over at the Airbender children. Their actions had put them in danger, but deep down, she was proud of them. They'd fought hard to protect their home.

26

Tenzin leaned forward anxiously in Oogi's saddle. The second he'd seen the Equalist airship hovering over Air Temple Island, he'd called his sky bison and headed straight for home.

Korra, Mako, Asami, and Bolin sat behind Tenzin in the saddle, eager to help him protect his family. As they flew over the island, signs of battle littered the shore. The stone steps leading to the main gate were damaged, and clusters of trees had been knocked down.

Tenzin landed Oogi in the courtyard in front of his house. He was instantly relieved to see Lin Beifong and his children. Beifong stood next to a row of Equalist prisoners with their hands tied behind their backs. She directed several White Lotus sentries to move the prisoners into the temple until help arrived.

"Thank goodness you're all right!" Tenzin said. He hopped down from Oogi's saddle and ran to his children. He swept them up in an enormous bear hug.

"We caught the bad guys!" Meelo chirped excitedly.

Tenzin shot Beifong a worried look. "You let them fight? Do you realize what could have happened?"

"I would have been toast if it weren't for your kids," Beifong admitted. "You should be proud. You taught them well."

Tenzin looked at his children's faces, full of pride.

"Go on, be with your wife," Beifong said, pointing toward the house.

Tenzin nodded and rushed inside. As soon as he entered, he heard an unexpected sound. It was a baby crying.

"Pema!" Tenzin called. He followed the sound, racing toward the bedroom at the back of the house. He ran into the room and stopped when he saw his wife. She was sitting up in bed, cradling a newborn baby in her arms.

"Tenzin," she whispered. There were tears of joy in her eyes.

"I'm here, Pema," Tenzin murmured. He moved to Pema's side and stared down in wonder at the baby.

"Our new son," she said gently. Pema handed the infant to Tenzin. He wrapped the baby in his arms and held him snug against his chest.

Tenzin gazed into his son's face. The baby's large,

bright eyes stared back at him. "Hello," he said softly.

Jinora, Ikki, and Meelo poked their heads into the room from the doorway. Tenzin noticed and called them over. "Come meet your new brother."

"A brother? Well, it's about time!" Meelo said. The three kids gathered close to Tenzin and Pema, eager to get a look at the newest addition to the family.

"Welcome! I'm Ikki, and this is Jinora and Meelo! We have a super-great family and we're so happy you're part of it!" Ikki leaned over and placed a kiss on the baby's cheek.

"What are you going to name him?" Jinora asked her parents. "Can I pick?"

"We already chose a name," Pema answered.

"Rohan," Tenzin said.

Beifong, Korra, and Mako stepped quietly into the room.

"I'm so sorry to interrupt, but more airships are coming," Korra said. She and Beifong exchanged a worried glance.

Ikki saw the troubled expression on her father's face. "Everything's not going to be fine. Is it, Daddy?"

Tenzin sighed deeply and held his infant son tighter against his chest.

In the courtyard outside the family's home, Tenzin gathered with Beifong and Team Avatar. Several Equalist airships drifted toward the island, casting dark shadows on the bay.

"What do you want to do, Tenzin?" Korra asked.

The Master Airbender drew in a deep breath, folded his arms across his chest, and tucked his hands into the loose sleeves of his robes. "I need to protect my family and get them as far away from this conflict as possible. If Amon got his hands on my children . . . I hate to even think of it."

"If you're leaving, then I'm going with you," Beifong said.

"But—"

"No arguments. You and your family are the last Airbenders. There's no way in the world I'm letting Amon take your bending away."

"Thank you, Lin," Tenzin said, touched. He turned to Korra. "I want you to leave this island and hide for the time being."

Korra straightened and put her hands on her hips. "I'm not giving up," she protested.

"I'm not asking you to. I've sent word to the United Forces. They will be here soon," Tenzin explained. "And once my family is safe, I will return. With the reinforcements, we can turn the tide in this war."

"What you're saying is we need to be patient." Korra dropped her defiant stance as the realization dawned on her.

Tenzin smiled. As his airbending pupil, patience had never come easily to Korra. He placed a hand on her shoulder. "You're learning well," he said.

A short while later, Tenzin's family was seated in Oogi's saddle along with Lin Beifong. Korra watched sadly as Tenzin took one last look at the Air Temple and prepared to climb onto his sky bison. It was hard to believe they were leaving the island. Ever since Korra had arrived in Republic City, Air Temple Island had been her home. But perhaps even more importantly, Tenzin's family had become her family.

Korra waved goodbye to Pema and the children and hugged Tenzin firmly. He was more than just her airbending master; he was a friend.

"Stay safe, Korra," he said gently.

"You too," she replied.

"Tenzin, if we're leaving, we had better do it now," Beifong said, pointing. The Equalist airships were floating dangerously close to the shoreline.

Tenzin hopped up onto Oogi's neck and took the

sky bison's reins. He guided the huge creature into the air and flew out over the bay. Two more sky bison followed, carrying the Air Acolytes. The island was deserted except for Team Avatar and a small troop of White Lotus sentries.

Suddenly, two of the approaching Equalist airships changed course. They made wide turns, engines whirring, and sped after the family of Airbenders. Korra watched from below, wanting to help Tenzin, but she had troubles of her own.

A third airship stopped over the island's rocky beach and launched a grappling cable. Within minutes, a group of Chi-blockers had swung onto the zip line and slid to the ground. The White Lotus sentries ran down from their posts and closed ranks in front of Korra.

"Go!" said the captain. "We'll hold them off!"

Korra nodded and whistled for Naga. The polar bear–dog bounded over the crest of a hill and met her in the courtyard outside the family's house. Mako, Asami, and Bolin raced out of the house at the sound of the commotion, and Korra urged them onto Naga's back. It was time to make their escape.

While the sentries clashed with the Equalist invaders, Korra led Naga down a twisting path toward the docks. The polar bear–dog galloped swiftly along the road, her nose alert for the scent of danger.

Naga's ears pricked up as she detected a faint rustling coming from the slope beside the path. All of a sudden, Amon's lieutenant dove off the steep hill and flipped down into the road. He landed directly in front of Team Avatar with his kali sticks blazing.

"The mustache guy!" Bolin shouted.

Naga roared and charged the Lieutenant. He crouched and whirled his sticks threateningly, but the polar bear–dog wasn't intimidated. She leapt into the air and swept a mighty paw at the Lieutenant, batting him from the path.

"Nice one, Naga!" Korra said, steering the polar bear–dog onto the docks. They raced to the end of the long pier and plunged into the water. Korra bent the water around them, enveloping Naga and the rest of Team Avatar in a large pocket of air. Naga swam deep into the waters of Yue Bay, headed for Republic City.

In the skies above the bay, Tenzin urged Oogi to go faster. The Equalist airships were gaining on them. Pema and the children huddled together in the back of the sky bison's saddle while Beifong studied the enemy ships. Sharp fins jutted from their round metal hulls, slicing through the clouds.

Within seconds, the ships pulled into striking distance. One of the zeppelins launched a long cable that whipped through the air. The cable snaked out toward Oogi and the end flared into a giant net.

Beifong reacted quickly, extending one of the cables from her armor to shred the net in half. She flung a second cord into the air and latched on to the ship's line. The former police chief glanced at Tenzin and his family and took a deep breath. If they were to have any hope of escaping, she was going to have to take those airships out.

"Whatever happens to me," she said, "don't turn back."

Tenzin's eyes widened as he took in the meaning of Beifong's words. "Lin, what are you doing?"

Beifong didn't answer. She ran down Oogi's tail and leapt into the sky. Swinging in a wide arc on the airship's line, she headed directly for the lead zeppelin. In midair, she retracted her cable and reeled herself in, landing on top of the ship's hull.

Beifong stomped the airship's metal shell. A fierce vibration rang out from beneath her foot, tearing a huge rift in the hull. She gestured with her arms, widening the split until an enormous hole gaped in the side of the craft. Beifong ran along the top of the ship and peeled the metal away in one huge sheet. A loud boom sounded beneath her feet as smoke belched from the hole and the entire airship began to fall.

Beifong jumped from the ship, using a torn piece of metal as a springboard. She rocketed through the air and landed on top of the second zeppelin. The former chief stomped again, pulling metal apart, but this time the ship's crew was ready for her. Two Chi-blockers climbed through a hatch onto the hull and threw their electrified bolas. The weapons thudded into Beifong with a jolt of electricity. She cried out and crumpled into unconsciousness.

The airship's propellers changed direction and the craft banked slowly. It turned away from Tenzin and his family, floating back toward Air Temple Island.

From Oogi's saddle, Tenzin, Pema, and their children watched in sorrow as Beifong was taken prisoner.

"That lady is my hero," Meelo said softly.

Tenzin nodded, blinking tears from his eyes. "Yes, she is."

Night had fallen on Air Temple Island by the time Beifong was brought before Amon. The Equalist leader stood in the courtyard outside Tenzin's house, flanked by his lieutenant, Hiroshi Sato, and a troop of Chi-blockers.

Amon stared down through his mask at Republic City's former chief of police. Her arms and legs were bound in platinum shackles, and even though she'd been pushed down to her knees, she stared up at him with defiance.

"Tell me where the Avatar is and I'll let you keep your bending." Amon's voice was silky with menace.

"I won't tell you anything, you monster!" Beifong hissed.

"Very well," Amon said curtly. He had no time for games. He fixed his clawlike hands on Beifong's face, then touched a single finger to her forehead. Her eyes widened as the energy drained from her body. She went rigid and screamed in shock. The scream faded into the night as the former police chief slumped to the ground.

On the deck of a battleship several days' journey from Republic City, a young officer brought a very important message to his commander.

"General, I just received a wire from the Avatar. She says Amon and his forces have gained control of the city. How do you want to respond?"

General Iroh turned his gaze from the ocean to the officer in front of him. A look of determination settled across his rugged features. He bore more than a passing resemblance to his grandfather, Fire Lord Zuko.

"Tell the Avatar we will be arriving in three days' time and that I look forward to winning back Republic City together."

"As you wish, General Iroh." The officer bowed and took his leave.

General Iroh turned his eyes back to the sea. Around him, the entire naval fleet of the United Forces floated steadily in battle formation. The Avatar was depending on him, and he wasn't about to let her down.

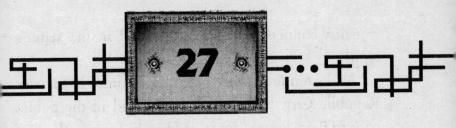

27

It had only been two days since Amon had taken control of Republic City, but in that short time he'd transformed it dramatically. A fleet of Equalist airships patrolled the city's skies, while troops of mecha-tanks prowled the streets below. Huge propaganda posters and banners hung from all the city's major buildings. Amon's face was draped across city hall and police headquarters, his hollow eyes trapping citizens in their cruel glare.

The streets were no longer safe for benders, who were arrested on sight, rounded up by Chi-blockers, and taken away. No one knew where they were being held.

In a blatant display of his power, Amon desecrated the tall stone statue of Avatar Aang that kept watch over the bay with his own image. He placed a mask that matched his own over the Avatar's features and draped

Equalist banners from the stone staff in the statue's hands.

As the ominous specter of Amon loomed larger over Republic City, loyal Equalists gathered in the public park to hear devoted Equalist Hiroshi Sato speak.

"It is a glorious day, my Equalist brothers and sisters!" Sato said. "Amon has torn down the tyrannical bending government and declared bending illegal! He has the Avatar on the run!"

The crowd roared in approval. Hiroshi smiled down at them from the stage in the center of the park. He was flanked by Amon's lieutenant and a group of masked Chi-blockers.

"One day soon, bending will no longer exist, and we will live in a world where everyone is finally equal! The United Forces are on their way right now to try to stop that dream, but we will prevail!" Hiroshi shouted.

The crowd went wild, cheering loudly. Two of the Chi-blockers near the front of the stage exchanged a glance. They broke ranks with the others and slipped off behind a line of hedges at the edge of the square.

One of the Chi-blockers stomped the ground and a hole opened up in the earth. The two Equalists slipped through the hole into an underground tunnel. Seconds later, the hole closed above their heads and they stripped off their masks.

"How do the Chi-blockers breathe in these things?" Mako asked. He stared at the mask in his hands, relieved to be free of the disguise at last.

Korra exhaled an impatient breath, blowing her bangs out of her eyes. The mask had pulled her hair loose. "Can you believe Hiroshi?" she asked, ignoring Mako's question. "'The Avatar's on the run.' I'm not running from anyone."

Mako raised an eyebrow, noting the edge in Korra's voice.

"Let's go back up there and knock some heads!" she said. "They'll never know what hit 'em."

Mako placed a hand on her arm. "Relax. General Iroh's coming with an entire fleet of battleships. Then Amon will be the one who's running."

"I hate this being patient stuff," Korra mumbled.

The left corner of Mako's mouth drew up in a lopsided grin. He reached out and tucked a few strands of hair behind her ear. "I know," he said softly.

Korra froze at the weird feeling she sometimes got when she was around Mako—like she was being pulled toward him. She shook it off and started walking farther into the tunnel. This wasn't the time or the place.

Mako followed, and soon the tunnel opened up into a network of secret caverns. They rounded a corner and walked into a large camp. Makeshift tents, shacks, and cooking fires dotted the space that most of Republic City's transients had come to call home.

Asami greeted them at the edge of the camp, but her greeting was far from pleasant. "You two were gone a while," she said icily.

"We were doing reconnaissance," Mako responded, annoyed.

"Whatever." Asami turned away.

Korra's stomach dropped. She didn't want to be the cause of tension between Mako and Asami.

"Welcome back!" a voice interrupted. The three of them turned to see a man approaching. His clothing was patched and worn and his scraggly gray hair stood out at odd angles on his head, but that did nothing to diminish his winning smile.

Immediately, Korra's mood lightened. Gommu was one of the very first people she'd met when she arrived in Republic City. At the time, he'd been living in a bush in the middle of the park, but since then, he'd taken up residence underground with the city's other vagabonds.

"I hope you've worked up an appetite," Gommu said, "because dinner is served."

He led Korra, Mako, and Asami to his cooking fire, where Bolin was already seated. Pabu chattered excitedly and climbed onto Bolin's shoulder.

Gommu moved to the fire and stirred a large pot of gruel.

"Thanks so much for letting us hide out with you down here the past few days," Korra said.

"Honored to oblige! My associates and I heartily oppose Amon's so-called Equalist policies," Gommu replied. He ladled out helpings of the gruel and passed worn tin bowls to everyone.

Bolin ate enthusiastically, but Asami eyed her bowl with suspicion. Strange lumps floated in the thick gruel. She thought about asking what was in it, but then decided it was probably better not to know.

Gommu shoveled a spoonful into his mouth and swallowed. "We got benders and non-benders living together down here. But do you see us fighting? No, siree. We figured out how to harmoniously coexist."

"You are wise and noble," Bolin said, "and this is the best street gruel I've ever tasted. Seriously."

Asami hesitantly put a spoonful into her mouth.

"Thank you," Gommu replied. "I culled it from the finest Dumpsters the city has to offer."

At the sound of his words, Asami retched, spitting the gruel back into her bowl. It was a far cry from dinners at the Sato mansion.

Later that night, the camp settled down to sleep. Cooking fires were extinguished and bedrolls unfurled. Korra sat with her back resting against Naga's side, waiting for sleep to come. After a couple of hours, it was clear that she was hopelessly awake.

"Can't sleep either?" Mako asked. He walked quietly toward Korra, stepping over sleeping bodies, and sat down next to her.

"No. I have this awful pit in my stomach," she answered.

"Me too." Mako ran his fingers nervously through his spiky, dark hair.

"It's so crazy." Korra breathed an anxious sigh. "A few months ago, I was in the South Pole, practicing for my firebending test, and now I'm in the middle of an all-out war."

"I know," Mako agreed. "We didn't even know each other then, and now I can't imagine my life without you in it."

Korra looked up at him, startled. Mako's eyes were steady as they met hers. "You're the most loyal, brave, and selfless person I've ever known," he said gently.

Part of him felt oddly calm now that he'd said it out loud. The other part felt nervous but exhilarated, which was usually how he felt around Korra. He leaned closer to her and the feeling got stronger, spiking along with his heartbeat.

"I think you're pretty incredible, too, but . . . you already knew that," Korra said. She'd told Mako how she felt a while ago, and he'd decided to date Asami. There were times when he'd seemed confused, like he didn't know which way his feelings would lead him, but there was no confusion in the tender way he looked at her now. Korra knew he was seeing things clearly for the first time.

If only she could say the same for herself. It was hard to think with Mako leaning toward her. He really was incredible—fierce and dark-eyed and gentle all at once. Korra felt it again, the feeling that he was somehow tugging her toward him. It made her breath catch in her throat and reminded her of the time they'd kissed. It was far too easy to remember what that kiss felt like—the excitement of it—and ignore the hurt she'd felt later when Mako had chosen Asami.

Suddenly, Korra blinked and turned away from him. "I should probably try to get some sleep," she said quickly.

Mako straightened and cleared his throat. "Me too." He dragged his gaze away from Korra's face, but not before she noticed the look of disappointment in his eyes. He climbed to his feet and began to walk back toward his bedroll.

"Good night," he said softly.

Air Temple Island was no longer the quiet, peaceful home to Tenzin's family and the Air Acolytes. Since they'd been forced to flee, Amon had taken over, making the island his base of operations. Equalist soldiers took up posts once manned by White Lotus sentries, and instead of winged lemurs and sky bison in the animal habitats, benders were being kept like beasts.

Amon stood in the courtyard outside Tenzin's house as the Lieutenant brought a shackled prisoner before him. The Lieutenant stripped off the man's blindfold and pushed him to his knees. Amon looked at the man, whose frightened eyes pleaded with him.

"You will now be cleansed of your impurity," the Equalist leader said. He fixed his clawlike grip on the man's face and, in a matter of seconds, took his bending away. The prisoner shuddered and collapsed to the ground. Several Chi-blockers dragged his limp body from the courtyard.

"Bring me the next bender," Amon told his lieutenant. A long line of shackled benders stretched across the courtyard and wound across the island to the animal habitats on the far shore. The Lieutenant took the next prisoner from the front of the line.

Soon no one would be able to bend. Amon would see to that, one bender at a time.

28

It was early morning when Team Avatar left the underground tunnels and climbed out of a drainage pipe near the docks. A thick fog had settled over the city, making the streets seem deserted.

Korra, Mako, Asami, and Bolin found an isolated concrete landing overlooking the bay and hunkered down to watch the sea. Bolin pulled a brass spyglass from his belt and scanned the horizon.

"Once the United Forces arrive, we need to be ready to help any way we can," Korra said. Team Avatar nodded in agreement, anxiously awaiting the reinforcements.

"They're here!" Mako said, pointing.

In the bay, a line of battleships emerged from the mist. They were impressive vessels with long, sturdy hulls and multiple decks. The decks were loaded with fire cannons and earth disks to be used by the bending members of the crew. At the front of each ship, two golden dragon figureheads extended from twin bows.

Korra breathed a small sigh of relief. The United Forces had finally arrived! Still, something nagged at her as she looked out over the waters of the bay.

"Wait a second. Where are the Equalist airships?" she asked.

The airships had been a constant presence ever since Amon had gained control of the city. They loomed over the skyline, throwing lengthy shadows over the streets below. Today, however, they were nowhere to be seen.

Mako frowned. He took the spyglass from his brother and ran to the edge of the landing. He scanned the shoreline and the streets surrounding the docks.

"I don't see any mecha-tanks either," he said uneasily.

At that same moment, aboard his battleship, General Iroh had a similar thought. He stood on the forward deck with two of his officers, staring at the unusually quiet city.

"Amon had to know we were coming," he said. "So why aren't we meeting any resistance?" The general walked over to the ship's rail, listening to the eerie silence. "Something's not right."

Just then, an explosion rocked a nearby vessel. Iroh turned in alarm and peered down into the waters lapping the hull of his ship. Deadly sea mines floated up from below. The spiky metal explosives bobbed on the surface of the waves, surrounding the fleet.

The mines drifted dangerously close to the battleships. Several of them collided with the vessels and exploded in a burst of flame. The powerful force of the explosions tore jagged holes in the hulls, instantly crippling a portion of the fleet.

"It's a trick!" General Iroh shouted. He raced onto the command bridge and relayed a series of orders through the ship's radio. "Water- and Earthbenders, detonate those mines!"

Across the fleet, the benders of the United Forces climbed to the decks. The Waterbenders stirred the waves, pushing the mines away from the ships. The Earthbenders drew rock disks from large dispensers on deck and flung them at the explosives, detonating them from a safe distance.

It was dangerous work, and it was interrupted by a loud buzzing overhead.

"What is that sound?" Iroh asked. He stepped out of the bridge and looked up at the sky. The droning grew louder and more insistent, like a swarm of buzzard-wasps.

From the landing on the docks, Team Avatar followed the strange noise. Mako turned the spyglass toward the sound and gasped. In the distance, Equalist aircraft appeared on the horizon, but they were nothing like the airships the team were used to seeing.

These were biplanes, nimble and light, with two fixed wings stacked on top of each other. Each plane had a large propeller engine in the nose, an open-air cockpit, and two smaller propellers at the ends of the wings.

"Where does Hiroshi find the time to keep inventing new evil machines?" Bolin asked, incredulous.

Korra's heart sank. Between the floating mines and the fighter planes, the United Forces battleships were trapped. She ran to the end of the landing and dove off the edge into the water below.

The squadron of biplanes streaked past the city skyline and flew out into the bay. They soared in a tight V formation, swooping low over the fleet. When they were directly overhead, they dropped bombs, which plummeted like stones, destroying some ships on impact and seriously damaging others. Smoke belched from the injured vessels and billowed into the sky.

The fighter planes flew in a wide arc and circled back for another bombing run. This time they dropped torpedoes, which splashed down into the bay and sped toward the ships with deadly accuracy.

29

As Korra swam toward the fleet, torpedoes streaked through the water around her. She flipped and dove, narrowly avoiding collision with the self-propelled bombs, but the heavy iron battleships weren't as lucky. The torpedoes struck them mercilessly in fiery explosions that rumbled across the bay.

Beneath the waves, Korra felt the impact of the blasts and quickly surfaced for air. With her head above water, she saw more Equalist biplanes approaching and knew she had to stop them. She dove again and swam deep.

Korra spiraled through the water, making it whirl around her. The swirling currents formed a powerful funnel. She reached out with her waterbending and reversed the direction of the whirlpool, channeling the water upward. Korra rode the funnel and rocketed out of the sea on a towering waterspout.

From the top of the spout, high above the water, Korra had a bird's-eye view of the battle. Firebenders, Earthbenders, and Waterbenders swarmed the decks of the few remaining battleships as several biplanes raced toward them. Korra reacted quickly, drawing a huge plume of water from the ocean and freezing it into a giant spike of ice. The ice spike slashed through the wing of a fighter plane, sending it tumbling through the air until it crashed into the ocean.

A second biplane flew directly into Korra's swirling funnel of water. The force of the spinning current crushed the aircraft before the funnel collapsed. Korra fell back into the sea, determined to help the United Forces from beneath the waves.

A torpedo shot past her on a collision course with the lead battleship. She sensed the flow of water and bent it, redirecting the torpedo back to the surface and into a biplane overhead. The plane exploded in a flash of fire and rained debris into the water.

On board the lead battleship, General Iroh climbed the main mast into the crow's nest. It was the tallest point on the ship, which made it the best place to fight incoming aircraft. A skilled Firebender, Iroh unleashed a barrage of fiery blasts into the sky. Four biplanes closed in on him, zigzagging through the air to avoid his fire strikes. The general lashed out again, releasing a long stream of flame. The fire swept across the sky, burning through the wings of an Equalist plane. The plane veered off and plummeted into the bay, but the remaining aircraft stayed on course. They swooped in over the ship and dropped three bombs in quick succession. The explosions thundered across the vessel, blasting Iroh from the crow's nest. He plunged into the water below, knocked unconscious by the fall.

Korra swam toward General Iroh. The Firebender's limp body sank like a stone, but she dove after him, grabbing the collar of his ruined uniform. Korra pulled the general into her arms and swam to the surface. She dragged him away from the thick of the fighting, swimming slowly toward the docks.

Moments later, General Iroh woke up.

"Avatar Korra?" he asked groggily.

"It's all right. I've got you," Korra answered.

"You saved my life," the general said. "Thank you."

Korra nodded grimly. The few battleships left were engulfed in flames and sinking fast. Despite the best efforts of the United Forces, the Equalists had won the battle of the bay.

Back at the underground camp, Korra tended to General Iroh's wounds. His arm had been injured in the fall from the crow's nest, and he'd sustained a number of cuts and scrapes. Mako, Asami, and Bolin sat quietly across from them, reflecting on the devastation of the battle.

"I was prepared to deal with Sato's mecha-tanks, but not these new high-speed aircraft," General Iroh said.

"I know." Korra nodded. "Every time we think we have an advantage in this war, Amon outsmarts us."

"No matter what our plan is, he always has a better one," Bolin said glumly.

General Iroh straightened. A look of determination settled on his features. "Amon is winning so far, but we're not out of the fight yet."

Bolin was taken with the general's defiant enthusiasm. "I like this man's confidence!" he said. "So, uh, how are we not out of the fight?"

"A second wave of reinforcements is on the way, but I need to warn them." General Iroh stood and flexed his injured arm. Korra's healing had done the trick. There was hardly any pain. "Do you still have a way to get a message out?" he asked.

"I know just the man for the job," Korra answered.

Gommu led the general and Team Avatar into a rough-and-ready communications shack behind his tent. A large map of Republic City was spread out across a rickety wooden table, and next to it, a telegraph machine had been rigged from odds and ends. Gommu himself had once been a telegraph operator and was eager to help the general.

"And who is the recipient of this message?" he asked. He sat in front of the telegraph machine, fingers poised over the transmitter.

"Commander Bumi, second division of the United Forces," Iroh said.

Korra's eyes widened. "You mean Tenzin's brother?"

The general nodded. "Yes. Bit of a wild man, but the bravest commander you'll ever meet."

"Ready, sir," Gommu said.

Iroh dictated his message advising Commander Bumi to retreat to a nearby island until he received word to approach the city. Gommu carefully tapped out the telegram, and within seconds, the message was sent. Satisfied, the general turned back to Team Avatar.

"Now comes the hard part. We need to ground those aircraft," he explained. "Otherwise, Bumi's fleet will never be able to retake the city."

Mako pointed to the map on the table. "They flew in from this direction. The airfield must be somewhere over this mountain range."

Iroh's brows drew together. The general was deep in thought, formulating a plan. "Everyone get ready," he said finally. "We leave at dawn."

General Iroh walked out of the shack with Mako, Asami, and Bolin. After the day's defeat, they were relieved that there was still hope of winning this war. Only Korra hung back, a thoughtful expression on her face.

"Wait," she called to them. Everyone stopped and turned to look at her. "I'm sorry, but I'm not going with you tomorrow."

"What?" Mako asked, concerned.

"Why not?" Asami said.

"I'm sick and tired of hiding from Amon. It's time I face him." Korra's mind was made up.

"That's not a good plan. We need to stick together," General Iroh advised.

Korra shook her head emphatically. "I'm not waiting for him to hunt me down. My gut's telling me it's time to end this—on my terms."

"Korra, this is not a mission you should be handling alone," the general warned her.

"She won't be." Mako walked over and stood beside her. "I'm going with you."

"You don't have to do that," Korra said.

"Yes, I do," Mako answered firmly.

Asami looked away, crushed.

The general scratched his chin, considering Korra's determination. At last, he heaved a heavy sigh. "My grandfather would respect the Avatar's instinct. So will I."

30

The next morning, the mood in the camp was somber as Team Avatar got ready to split up and head out on separate missions. Mako and Bolin hugged goodbye, and Korra bid farewell to Naga. The polar bear–dog would carry General Iroh, Asami, and Bolin into the mountains to find the hidden Equalist airfield.

Before they went their separate ways, Mako gently pulled Asami aside.

"I'm sorry things got so messed up between us," he said, "but whatever happens today, I want you to know how much I care about you."

"I care about you, too," Asami told him. She leaned in and kissed Mako softly on the cheek. Mako looked at her, startled. Even though neither of them said it, they both knew what had just happened. Asami had kissed Mako goodbye for good.

She backed away slowly and joined Bolin and

General Iroh. The three of them climbed onto Naga's back and disappeared into the network of tunnels.

Korra and Mako pulled on Chi-blocker uniforms for disguise and headed into a drainage pipe that led toward the docks.

Gommu watched everyone depart. He was sad to see them go but eager for them to succeed in the war against Amon.

"Good fortune and success to you, valiant heroes!" he shouted. His voice echoed through the tunnels, urging Team Avatar onward.

When Korra and Mako exited the pipe, they were right at the edge of Republic City. The waters of the bay lapped the shoreline just a few feet in front of them. They walked down into the water and Korra bent the waves, pushing them back to form a protective bubble of air around them.

Enclosed in the dome of air, she and Mako walked beneath the waters of the bay along the ocean floor. A short while later, they emerged on the rocky shores of Air Temple Island.

As they climbed onto the beach, they noticed an Equalist airship hovering next to the tall spire of the temple. A cable hung down from the underside of the ship. Slowly, it began to retract, drawing someone up into the gondola.

"That's Amon!" Korra whispered. Once the Equalist leader was on board, the ship banked and floated off toward the city.

"We need to get into the temple," Mako said quietly. "Then, when he returns—"

"We ambush him."

Korra and Mako pulled their Chi-blocker masks into place and ran along a trail that led to the temple. They had almost reached the front entrance when suddenly Amon's lieutenant stepped into their path.

"What are you two doing down here?" the Lieutenant asked.

Mako and Korra froze. They knew the Lieutenant couldn't have recognized them in their Chi-blocker uniforms, but they were still afraid of being found out.

"Uh, we were just transferred," Mako responded, thinking quickly.

"Well, you're getting transferred again. Amon wants extra security at the arena today," the Lieutenant said.

"The arena? For what?" asked Mako.

"The rally." The Lieutenant studied them carefully. "You should have been briefed about this."

"We'll be there, sir!" Korra bowed quickly. Satisfied

with her response, the Lieutenant dismissed her and Mako. They walked back toward shore, but as soon as the Lieutenant was out of sight, they circled around to the rear of the temple.

"I know another way in," Korra whispered.

She showed Mako a secret hatch in the low stone wall behind the building. They climbed into a crawl space that led to the temple's spire. Once inside, they peeled off their Chi-blocker masks.

"Let's hide in the attic until Amon comes back," Korra whispered.

Mako nodded, and they climbed a nearby ladder and emerged through a trapdoor in the attic floor. Mako's gaze drifted across the room as he entered. He stopped suddenly when his eyes fell on a shadowy figure.

"Uh . . . we're not alone up here," he said to Korra.

Korra looked up to see a man with tangled hair and tattered clothes sitting in a prison cell against the far wall. There was something familiar about him.

"Tarrlok?" she asked in shock.

The Bloodbender tilted his face and it caught the light. "I don't suppose you're here to rescue me?" he asked sourly.

"We had no idea you were here," Korra said. "Are there other prisoners on the island?"

"No, I'm the only one," Tarrlok answered.

"What makes you so special?" she asked sarcastically.

Tarrlok met Korra's gaze. A hint of anger simmered in his eyes.

"I'm Amon's brother," he confessed.

Mako and Korra stared at Tarrlok, stunned by his revelation. They walked closer to the prison cell and stopped just outside the iron bars.

Tarrlok pushed himself to his feet as he spoke. "Amon is from the Northern Water Tribe. He's a Waterbender and a Bloodbender, just like me."

"What?" Korra said. She and Mako looked at each other in surprise.

"Did you know this all along?" Mako asked Tarrlok.

"No," he answered. "Not until he captured me."

"He's a bender leading an anti-bending revolution!" Korra shook her head in disbelief.

"He has hidden his secret well. I believe that is why he is keeping me up here, away from his followers," Tarrlok explained.

Korra still couldn't quite believe it. "How did your brother end up becoming Amon?"

Tarrlok reached out and gripped the bars of his cell, resting his head against them. When he began his tale, his voice was weary. "It all began with my father, Yakone. . . ."

31

*A*fter Avatar Aang took Yakone's bending away, he was sent to prison. But that wasn't the end for the thin-faced criminal with the wicked smile. With the help of his former gang, he escaped and had surgery to alter his appearance.

With his new face, Yakone assumed a new identity. He settled in the frozen Northern Water Tribe lands and met a kind, caring young woman. Before long, they started a family together. Amon was the firstborn and was given the name Noatak. Three years later, Tarrlok was born.

For a while, the young family was happy. Tarrlok looked up to his older brother, a good-natured boy who always looked out for him. But things changed when the boys discovered they were Waterbenders.

At first, they were excited by their new abilities, but their training brought out a different side of their father. Something hardened in Yakone as he taught his sons. He was pleased with Noatak, who seemed to have a natural talent for waterbending, but Tarrlok wasn't as lucky.

Once, when Tarrlok was only five years old, Yakone scolded him for struggling through practice. Both boys balanced globes of water in the air, guiding them back and forth in a circular motion. Unfortunately, tiny drops of water leaked from Tarrlok's globe.

"Tarrlok, you better shape up or you'll be out here in the cold all night until you get it right!" Yakone shouted.

Tarrlok's face crumpled and his chin quivered. "I'm trying!" he wailed.

"Try harder! Your brother was never this sloppy!" Yakone said angrily.

Noatak felt bad for his little brother and placed a hand on his shoulder. "Dad, he'll get it. He just needs more time," he told their father.

Yakone was furious. He whirled on Noatak and fixed him with a hard look. "Don't talk back to me, son. Ever."

Two years later, Yakone took his sons on a hunting trip far outside their village. It was then that he revealed his true identity as Republic City's most notorious crime boss. He also explained that he had once been an extremely talented Bloodbender.

"What's bloodbending?" young Tarrlok asked.

"The most powerful and feared form of bending in the world," Yakone answered. "It was declared illegal, thanks to that coward Katara, but our family has the strongest line of Bloodbenders in history. You boys have this power inside of you, and I will teach you to master it."

"What happened to your bending, Dad?" Noatak asked hesitantly.

A dark expression clouded Yakone's features. "The Avatar stole it from me. That's why I brought you out here—to learn your destiny."

Tarrlok and Noatak stared at their father in fearful awe.

"You two will become Bloodbenders of the highest order. When the time is right, you will claim Republic City, and you will destroy the Avatar." Yakone leaned down and looked directly into each son's eyes in turn. "You must avenge me. That is your purpose in life."

From that moment on, everything changed for the worse. The family's happy days were over.

Every full moon, Yakone took his sons on more hunting trips, where he secretly taught them to bloodbend. At first, he had them practice the ability on animals. Tarrlok never *forgot the day he saw his brother bloodbend an arctic yak.*

Noatak took a deep breath and hooked his fingers in the air, curling them inward as if plucking invisible strings. The yak's body seized and its eyes rolled in fear. Noatak forced the animal to rear back and stand on its hind legs. Tarrlok gasped, as frightened as the yak appeared to be.

Yakone scowled at his youngest son. "Toughen up, Tarrlok. You'll need a thicker skin for this."

Tarrlok looked away in sorrow. Noatak finally released the yak from his bloodbending grip and the creature darted away. Yakone placed a hand on Noatak's shoulder and beamed with pride.

A few years later, Yakone taught his sons to bloodbend without the need of the full moon. He drove the brothers relentlessly to master the dark bending skill. Noatak flourished, reveling in his newfound power, but Tarrlok hated every minute of it.

One day, Yakone insisted that Tarrlok bloodbend a pack of wolves that had gathered in a clearing just outside their village. Reluctantly, Tarrlok extended his arms, fingers sawing, clawlike, through the air. The wolves grew rigid and howled in protest. Tarrlok manipulated their furry bodies, controlling the flow of the blood inside them. They whined as he marched them back and forth across the clearing. Their paws struck the snow in jerky steps and their bodies swayed in an unnatural dance.

Yakone nodded and Tarrlok released the wolves, relieved to relinquish his hold over them. With their tails tucked between their legs, the animals ran off, but Noatak stood and stopped them. By this time, he had mastered Yakone's more powerful psychic bloodbending technique. He simply stared at the wolves and the entire pack froze in midstep.

Noatak dragged the wolves back toward himself. Their paws scrabbled on the snow at first, but eventually, all resistance faded. Noatak pressed the animals back onto their hind legs so that they stood as rigid as statues. Then he levitated the entire pack into the air.

Yakone's eyes brightened with evil glee. With a single breath, Noatak lowered the wolves to the ground and forced them to bow down on their front paws. Whimpering, the pack knelt at his feet as if he were their king.

"That's the way it's done!" Yakone said. "That's what you need to strive for, Tarrlok!"

Noatak released the wolves and walked off alone into the snow. Even though he was the favorite, things weren't easier for him. He carried the heavy burden of all Yakone's expectations and demands.

Noatak didn't fare well under the pressure of his father's expectations. He grew cold and detached. He was no longer the devoted older brother Tarrlok had loved and admired. His face was blank as he went about his daily chores, and on the rare occasion when he chanced to smile, it never reached his eyes.

Yakone continued his ruthless training, pushing both of his sons to extremes. One day, he made them bloodbend each other. Snow whirled around the brothers as they faced off. Noatak went first, pinning his younger brother with his bloodbending gaze. Tarrlok's body grew rigid with pain. He struggled in Noatak's psychic grip.

Tarrlok cried out in pain as Noatak increased the pressure of his grasp. He bent his younger brother's body backward toward the ground. Enjoying the exercise, Yakone allowed Tarrlok to writhe in pain a few moments more before he signaled to his older son to stop. Noatak released his hold. His eyes were empty.

"Tarrlok, your turn," Yakone ordered.

Tarrlok drew in a shaky breath and pushed himself to his feet. "No, I won't do it," he said. His voice was shaky with unshed tears.

"Bloodbend your brother, Tarrlok!" Yakone insisted.

"*That felt awful! I don't want to do that to anyone! I never want to bloodbend again!*" Tarrlok shouted.

Yakone's eyes narrowed in rage. He marched toward Tarrlok threateningly. "*You're a disgrace and a weakling! I'll teach you a lesson, you insubordinate——*"

Yakone's words choked in his throat as Noatak stepped in front of his younger brother, shielding him. He fixed his father in his bloodbending gaze, seizing control of his body and holding him rooted to the spot.

"*How dare you bloodbend me?*" Yakone ground out through clenched teeth. A vein throbbed in his temple as he battled his son's powerful grasp.

"*What are you going to do about it?*" Noatak asked. His voice was eerily calm. "*You're the weak one.*" His eyes flashed as he forced his father to his knees. "*You always say bloodbending is the most powerful thing in the world, but it isn't—the Avatar is. He took your bending away. What could be more powerful than that?*"

Yakone roared, livid. "*I made you what you are! You're mine!*"

"*We're your sons, not your tools of revenge!*" Noatak said angrily. He turned to his little brother. "*Let's go. We can run away from him. Forever.*"

Frightened, Tarrlok hesitated. "*Run away? But what about Mom? We can't just leave her.*"

Noatak shook his head, disappointed. His lips curled

up in a sneer of disgust. "He was right about you. You are a weakling."

With a single sweep of his arm, Noatak tossed Yakone into a drift of snow and took off running into the swirling blizzard.

Yakone and Tarrlok searched for him for days, but Noatak had vanished without a trace. They believed he had perished in the storm.

Tarrlok looked up through the bars of his jail cell at Korra and Mako and sighed. "My mother was never the same after the loss of my brother, and neither was my father. He stopped training me. With Noatak gone, his hopes for revenge withered, and he passed away a few years later."

Korra shook her head, saddened. So much abuse—it was heartbreaking.

"Avatar Korra, I am truly sorry for all that I did to you," Tarrlok apologized. "I thought I was better than my father, but his ghost still shaped me. I became a soldier of revenge, just like he wanted me to be. And so did my brother."

Tarrlok hung his head. "The revolution may be

built on a lie, but I think Amon truly believes bending is the source of all evil in the world," he explained.

"How did you figure out Amon is your brother?" Mako asked.

"When he took my bending, the sensation was somehow familiar. I later recognized it as my brother's bloodbending grip," Tarrlok answered.

"So . . . he somehow uses bloodbending to take away people's bending?" Korra asked.

"I don't know how he does it," Tarrlok said, "but then again, I've never encountered a bender as strong as Noatak."

Korra frowned in thought. "How in the world do we beat him?"

"We can't," Mako said. "Any attack we throw at him he'll redirect with his mind. That's how he's been able to challenge any bender."

Korra nodded in agreement. Now there was no way they could go through with their original plan to ambush Amon when he returned to the temple. They would have to figure out something else.

Korra began to pace the room, thinking up a plan. After several moments, she had an idea. She stopped pacing, and Mako looked at her expectantly.

"This whole time, Amon has been one step ahead of us," Korra said. "But finally we have the advantage.

We know the truth about him. If we expose him as a bender in front of all his supporters—"

"At the rally!" Mako added, remembering the Lieutenant's words.

"—we could take away his true power," Korra pointed out.

"And undermine this whole revolution!" Eager to get started, Mako headed over to the trapdoor in the floor of the attic.

Korra followed but turned back to take one last look at Tarrlok. "We can't just leave him here," she told Mako.

Tarrlok shook his head, his eyes full of sadness and regret.

"Go," he said gravely. "Amon can't know anyone spoke to me. Defeat him. Put an end to this sad story."

32

In the snowcapped mountains outside Republic City, Naga emerged from the woods carrying General Iroh, Asami, and Bolin. The three of them climbed down from Naga's back and studied their surroundings. Up ahead was a low ridge with a steep canyon on the other side.

General Iroh looked up as a low-flying biplane dove into the canyon. He nodded to the others and they ran over to the ridge. When they looked down into the canyon, they spotted an enormous hangar.

"I think we found our secret airfield," the general said. "Bolin, once we get down there, I need you to tear up the runways. We can't let those aircraft take off."

"Aye-aye, Captain," Bolin replied. "Er . . . I mean, General."

Asami drew in a nervous breath. She knew that following the trail of the biplanes would lead directly to the man who had invented them—her father. But it was time to put a stop to his plans.

General Iroh noticed a rocky path leading down into the canyon. He motioned for Bolin and Asami to follow, and the three of them set out along the path. Giant metal fence posts rose from the ground just a few feet ahead on either side of the trail.

"Why would there be fence posts but no fence?" Asami wondered aloud. Before either the general or Bolin could respond, the three of them walked straight into an invisible electric fence. The electricity arced through their bodies in a painful shock, which knocked them unconscious.

Wearing their Chi-blocker disguises, Korra and Mako sneaked into the Pro-bending Arena for Amon's rally. The newly repaired building was hardly recognizable. Every available surface was covered in propaganda posters. The place was swarming with Chi-blockers and Equalist supporters who had gathered to hear Amon speak.

From their position in the referees' box overlooking the ring below, Korra and Mako watched as Amon rose on a platform in the bottom of the stage. He stepped forward through a dramatic cloud of smoke, which cleared as he lifted his arms. The crowd roared, and the Equalist leader signaled for quiet.

"Thank you all for joining me on this historic occasion," Amon said, addressing the audience. "When I was a boy, a Firebender struck down my entire family and left me scarred. That tragic event began my quest to equalize the world."

"That's a lie, Amon!" Korra's voice rang. She and Mako pulled off their Chi-blocker masks, revealing their faces. "Or should I call you Noatak."

Confusion rippled through the crowd.

Onstage, Amon stilled. The Lieutenant rushed to his side, leading a couple of Chi-blockers. "You want her taken out?" he asked.

Amon's eyes narrowed ominously behind his mask. After a moment, he spoke. "No. Everyone calm down. We have nothing to fear from the Avatar. Let's hear what she has to say."

Korra ran to the rail of the referees' stand and leaned out to speak to the crowd. "Amon has been lying to you. The Spirits didn't give him the power to take people's bending away—he uses bloodbending to do it. Amon is a Waterbender!"

"You're desperate, Avatar. Making up stories about me is a pathetic last resort," Amon said from the stage.

"Your family wasn't killed by a Firebender." Korra paused, then directed her words to the audience. "His father was Yakone! And his brother is Councilman Tarrlok!"

The crowd buzzed uneasily.

A sense of unease crept up the Lieutenant's back. His loyalty to Amon was unwavering, yet the Avatar's accusation gave him pause. He couldn't help but wonder why his leader treated Tarrlok differently than the other prisoners.

Amon remained calm. "An amusing tale," he said evenly. "But I will show you the truth." The Equalist leader lowered his hood and unfastened the straps that held his mask in place.

Slowly, he let the mask fall way to reveal his face.

"This is what a Firebender did to me!" Amon shouted.

The audience gasped as they stared at Amon's ruined face. Burns stood out in angry red welts across his skin. The scarred flesh was a stark contrast to his icy blue eyes.

The crowd grumbled. In the face of such clear evidence, there was only one way to explain the situation—the Avatar was lying. A chorus of boos swelled from the stands.

Korra reeled in shock. "No, I'm telling you . . . he's

a Waterbender!" she yelled desperately. She glanced at Mako, who studied Amon through narrowed eyes. "They don't believe me. It didn't work!"

"We said what we had to," Mako whispered urgently. "Let's get out of here."

Korra nodded. She and Mako backed toward the rear of the referees' stand.

"I wouldn't yet, Avatar. You'll miss the main event," Amon taunted them, carefully replacing his mask.

Just then, a trapdoor slid open in the stage. A platform rose, carrying four familiar prisoners. Tenzin, Jinora, Ikki, and Meelo were gagged and shackled to metal posts.

Korra's eyes widened in horror. "No! They got away. We saw them get away!"

Amon walked slowly toward the prisoners, savoring the fear he'd heard in the Avatar's voice. "Tonight, I rid the world of airbending! Forever!"

When Asami woke up, she found herself in an unfamiliar prison cell with General Iroh and Bolin. She was lying on the floor, and her hands were tied behind her back. Groggily, she pushed herself to a sitting position.

The general and Bolin were still unconscious. They were tied back to back, slumped against the bars of the cell.

"Asami!" a voice called.

She glanced up to see her father standing outside the cell. He looked down at her sadly. Regret filled his eyes.

"Asami, I know I have hurt you, and I am sorry. But I believe that one day, you will come to your senses and we can be a family again," Sato said.

Asami shook her head in a mixture of sorrow and anger. "Are you insane?" she asked. "How can we be a family after everything you've done? Mom would hate you for what you've become!"

General Iroh and Bolin stirred at the sound of Asami's raised voice.

Hiroshi's brows drew together in a dark scowl. "How dare you, Asami! I'm avenging her death!" he said furiously.

A Chi-blocker walked into the corridor outside the cell, interrupting them.

"The airplanes are ready for takeoff, sir," he told Hiroshi.

"Good. Annihilate the fleet."

General Iroh and Asami exchanged a worried glance. The fate of the four nations was in peril.

"That's right, General," Hiroshi said. "I intercepted your message to Commander Bumi. I know exactly where they're hiding." With that, Sato stepped back from the cell and turned on his heel, following the Chi-blocker down the corridor.

Asami was glum as she watched her father retreat.

"How are we going to get out of here?" she asked.

General Iroh craned his neck, staring over his shoulder at Bolin. "I don't suppose you know how to metalbend?" he asked hopefully.

"That is a negative, sir," Bolin replied.

Suddenly, the three of them heard a loud roar. Bolin turned his head toward the sound.

"Naga!" he exclaimed.

The polar bear–dog burst through the door at the end of the corridor. She bounded down the hall and stopped outside the prison cell. Naga sniffed and took a long look at the bars. Then she reared back on her hind legs and smashed the cage with her powerful front paws. Within seconds, the bars were reduced to a twisted mass of metal.

Bolin whooped gleefully. "Who needs a Metalbender? We've got Naga!"

With Naga's help, General Iroh, Asami, and Bolin worked free of their bonds and raced outside. They were in the middle of the airfield, with the large hangar just a few yards away. In the distance, six biplanes took off from the end of a long runway.

"I'm going after those aircraft!" Iroh said. The team nodded in agreement and split up. Bolin took Naga to destroy the runways, and Asami ran toward a row of empty mecha-tanks lined up outside the hangar.

She climbed into the open cockpit of one of the tanks and glanced at the controls. A slow smile spread over her face as she recognized the familiar levers and gauges. The tank worked just like a Future Industries forklift. Asami strapped herself into the pilot's seat and powered up the tank.

General Iroh ran to the end of the runway and kicked off from the ground. He propelled himself into the air on jets of flame shooting from his hands and feet. Iroh rocketed through the sky, closing fast on the last of the six fighter planes. He tucked his arms and legs closer to his body, gaining speed. Within seconds, he overtook the plane and dropped onto its top wing.

Iroh scrambled forward, fighting the wind, and dove into the cockpit. He wrestled the pilot, grappling with the man in the tiny space, until he succeeded in tossing him from the plane. The pilot opened his parachute and floated down into the mountains below.

General Iroh gripped the control stick and struggled with the unfamiliar steering mechanism. He was determined to do his best to save the Fleet and the Four Nations. The biplane wobbled unsteadily across the sky.

33

Korra raced to the front of the referees' stand in the Pro-bending Arena. On the stage below, Amon strode toward Tenzin and his family, eager to take their bending away.

"Amon, let them go!" Korra shouted.

"You're welcome to come down here and try to stop me," the Equalist leader said smoothly.

Korra leapt forward, but Mako held her back.

"He's trying to bait you," he warned.

"I don't care! We have to save them!" she said frantically.

"The Avatar needs to be reminded of the power I possess!" Amon told the crowd. He stretched his hands toward Tenzin, who struggled against his metal shackles. Jinora, Ikki, and Meelo shuddered with fear.

Mako leaned from the referees' box and shot a bolt of lightning directly at Amon. The blast knocked him across the stage into the Lieutenant and the other Chi-blockers.

Korra and Mako jumped over the rail of the referees' box and sprinted along the edge of the stands, headed for the stage. They pelted Amon and his henchmen with a steady barrage of fire strikes, driving them away from Tenzin and his family.

Korra landed on the stage and immediately ran to Tenzin, while Mako kept the Equalists at bay with firebending. After a quick glance at Tenzin's shackled hands, Korra set to work melting the chains with a concentrated beam of fire.

"Where are Pema and the baby?" she asked, slipping the gag from Tenzin's mouth.

"In prison," he answered.

"Beifong?"

"I don't know." Tenzin shook his head.

Korra returned her focus to the beam of fire and burned through the last bit of chain. Tenzin's hands sprang free. He leapt forward and fell in beside Mako, who was busy holding off Amon and his Chi-blockers.

Tenzin lashed out with a wide sweep-kick of air. The blast slammed into Amon and the Equalists, knocking them headlong off the stage. They tumbled awkwardly into the panicked crowd, which had begun to push toward the exits.

Korra finished freeing the kids and quickly led them into the hallway behind the stage. Moments later, Tenzin and Mako followed. They raced to the end of the hall, which split in two directions.

"Get the children out of here," Korra said to Tenzin. "We'll create a diversion."

Tenzin nodded and turned to his kids. "Let's go get your mother and the baby!"

"Prison break!" Meelo shouted.

The family of Airbenders took off down the emptiest corridor to avoid the panicking crowd and Amon's soldiers.

Korra and Mako barely had time to turn in the opposite direction when a door from the stage swung open. Amon stepped into the hall, his cold eyes settling immediately on the two of them.

Korra spun and unleashed a plume of fire. The flames crackled along the corridor, temporarily blocking Amon's path. She and Mako didn't waste a single second. They ran farther down the hall, searching for a way to escape.

Up ahead, Mako spotted the door to the old practice gym, and he and Korra ducked inside. The gym looked different now that the Equalists had taken over the arena. The equipment had been cleared out. Instead, there were wooden crates pushed up against the walls and pieces of old furniture stacked haphazardly around the room. Korra and Mako split up, finding separate places to hide.

In the hallway, Amon jumped through the flames, determined to hunt down the Avatar. He sped along the corridor until it came to a dead end. There was no sign of her or her Firebender friend.

Amon spun around. They couldn't have escaped so quickly. He studied the hallway and noticed one of the doors swinging closed. The Equalist leader smiled behind his mask. He had them now.

Amon walked slowly into the gym. Korra heard his footsteps echo across the floor. She was tucked under a table hidden beneath an old tarp. She couldn't see Amon, but she could hear him. She held her breath as the footsteps drew closer and stopped a few feet away.

Korra stayed perfectly still, listening for any sign of movement. She was rigid with fear. A cold sweat broke out on her forehead. After what seemed like forever, the footsteps started up again, drifting away from her hiding place.

Relieved, Korra let out a breath, but suddenly her body seized, caught in the grip of Amon's bloodbending. She screamed in pain, her limbs buckling, as he hauled her from her hiding place. The Equalist leader crushed her in his terrible bloodbending hold.

"Let her go!" Mako yelled.

He leapt out from behind a wall of wooden crates, blasting away at Amon with rapid bursts of fire. Amon easily dodged his strikes, then tilted his head toward Mako. The Firebender shuddered at the strange, skin-crawling sensation that made his limbs rigid with pain.

Amon raised his arms, levitating Mako and Korra. They writhed under the crippling pressure of his power, their arms and legs bent at unnatural angles. Then Amon dropped his arms swiftly, slamming Korra and Mako to the ground.

Mako struggled to climb to his feet, but Amon held him down. Mako watched in horror as the Equalist leader forced Korra to her knees.

Amon stood over the Avatar, looking down into her frightened eyes. He fixed his clawlike hands on her face.

"No!" Korra shouted wildly. Her heart was pounding so loudly she could barely hear her own voice. This wasn't supposed to happen. She'd had nightmares about this moment—the moment when Amon took her bending away for good. But they were just nightmares; they weren't supposed to come true.

Amon's eyes narrowed behind his mask. He reached out and pressed a single finger to Korra's forehead. She screamed and shuddered as the impossible happened.

The energy inside her flared and then burned out, her connection to the elements broken.

"I told you I would destroy you," Amon hissed.

It was done. The Avatar's bending was gone.

34

By the time the Equalist biplanes reached Yue Bay, General Iroh had learned the basics of keeping his plane in the air. He swooped down through the clouds and fell in behind the squadron of five fighter planes as they streaked out over the water.

Iroh leaned hard on the throttle and closed in on the enemy aircraft. Soon he was within striking distance. The general leaned forward in the open-air cockpit and shot a bolt of lightning from the tips of his fingers. The lightning arced across the sky and scored a direct hit on the nearest plane. The aircraft's engine sputtered and rattled to a halt.

General Iroh watched as the plane fell into a nosedive and spiraled toward the bay. On the way down, it collided with another biplane in a fiery explosion. Both pilots managed to parachute to safety before the wreckage plummeted into the water.

The general looked away from the crash and turned his focus to the three remaining planes. They zigzagged in front of him, their wings slicing through the clouds. One of the pilots pulled a lever and released an electrified bola from the rear of his plane. It whirled through the air and tangled in Iroh's propeller. The heavy spinning blades ground to a stop. Electricity crackled through the plane's engine, causing the controls to sizzle and spark.

General Iroh might have been new to flying, but he knew a bad sign when he saw one. He stood up in the cockpit and jumped out of the plane seconds before it exploded. He fell through the air, extending his arms and legs to slow his speed.

The general watched as two of the biplanes dipped and cut through the clouds below him. He tucked his arms and legs in close to his body and propelled himself forward on a burst of flame. Soon he landed with a thud on the top wing of one of the planes.

Iroh grabbed the wing with one hand and took aim at the biplane flying ahead of him. He launched a jet of fire, which rippled through the air and struck the enemy's engine. Smoke billowed from the plane as it tumbled through the sky.

In a flash, the general scrambled off the wing and slid down into the cockpit. He struggled briefly with the pilot before tossing him overboard. General Iroh grabbed the controls and scanned the horizon for the last plane. Suddenly, he heard the roar of engines overhead. He looked up just in time to see the last Equalist aircraft release a bomb directly above him.

The general pushed forward on the throttle, hoping to outrun the bomb, but it was too late. The heavy shell clipped the tail of the plane and exploded into flames. The plane shuddered and began to lose altitude, trailing black smoke.

General Iroh glanced up at the biplane. The cargo doors on the underside of the craft fell open and another bomb dropped into sight. Iroh stood up in the cockpit again and blasted the plane with a fiery burst. The bomb exploded, engulfing the aircraft in a rush of smoke and flames.

The general turned back to his own plane and struggled with the controls, but it was no use. He was on a collision course with the huge statue of Avatar Aang in the middle of the bay. At the last possible moment, he jumped from the cockpit and caught hold of the Equalist banner hanging from the statue's staff. The banner ripped under his weight and he was left dangling on a shred of cloth high above the water.

Iroh's plane crashed directly into the statue's head and exploded. The crash dislodged the Equalist mask covering the Avatar's features. Once again, Aang's face looked out over the bay.

General Iroh couldn't help but chuckle. "Thanks for looking out for me, Aang."

At the hidden Equalist airfield in the mountains, Bolin tore up slabs of earth, destroying the runways. He was eager to do his part to keep the enemy aircraft on the ground. But it wasn't long before the Equalists noticed and mounted a counterattack. Three mecha-tanks rolled toward him from the hangar, each of them launching grappling claws with incredible speed.

The claws snaked out toward Bolin at the end of their long cables, weaving through the air. Naga leapt in front of him and caught the cables between her powerful jaws. The polar bear–dog yanked them back and forth, jerking the mecha-tanks this way and that until they toppled over in a pile of twisted metal.

"Whoa, thanks, Naga!" Bolin said, impressed.

While Naga and Bolin continued to demolish the runways, Asami was inside the hangar, smashing empty biplanes in her mecha-tank.

"Asami, what do you think you're doing?" Hiroshi Sato's amplified voice interrupted.

Asami looked through the glass portholes in the dome of her armored suit to see her father strapped inside a mecha-tank. The two tanks faced each other across the hangar.

"You are aiding the very people who took your mother away!" Hiroshi shouted.

"You don't feel love for Mom anymore," Asami said angrily. "You're too full of hatred!"

"You ungrateful, insolent child!" Hiroshi bellowed. Furious, he set his tank in motion, rumbling toward his daughter. Asami launched both grappling claws at her father, but Hiroshi maneuvered around them. He barreled into Asami and sent her flying.

The mecha-tank landed on its back, jarring Asami in the cockpit. She struggled at the controls, trying to push the tank upright, but her father didn't give her the chance. He advanced until he towered over her and leveled his giant claws with a hydraulic hiss.

Hiroshi swung his claws wildly at Asami's tank, shattering the portholes and denting the cockpit. Asami covered her face with her arms, protecting herself from the falling glass.

"I now see there is no chance to save you!" Hiroshi roared. Just as he raised one enormous robotic arm and drew back to deliver his final blow, a huge boulder sailed through the air and smashed into his tank with a clang. Bolin charged into the hangar, riding on Naga's back. He punched the air, churning up huge slabs of rock from the ground and launching them at Hiroshi.

"Mister Sato, *you* are a horrible father!" Bolin shouted.

Asami took advantage of the distraction and guided her armored suit back to its feet. She reached out with grasping pincers, grabbed Hiroshi's tank, and threw it across the hangar. Asami rolled toward her father and used her tank's metal claws to pry open the cockpit of his machine.

Hiroshi looked up at her, wild-eyed, before he jumped out of his tank and ran from his daughter. With a heavy heart, Asami launched an electrified bola. The spinning metal disk whipped through the air, extending sparking cords that wrapped around Hiroshi. The shock of the current rippled through him and knocked him out. His body slumped to the ground.

Asami sighed and wiped a tear from her cheek. "You really are a horrible father," she whispered.

35

"**F**inally, you are powerless," Amon said.

He looked down at the Avatar. She was doubled over on the ground in front of him, struggling to push herself up to her knees.

Korra dragged her body forward and swung her arms weakly at Amon, but for the first time in her life, nothing happened. The earth beneath her remained still. The air hung motionless, and she could no longer hear the waters singing in the bay. She was cold. There was no heat, no energy inside her from which to create fire. She'd lost her link to the elements. Her power was gone.

Mako watched, devastated, as Korra collapsed to the floor at Amon's feet. He was caught in the Bloodbender's agonizing grip, which kept him pinned to the ground.

"Amon!" cried a voice.

The Equalist leader turned to see his Lieutenant approach from behind him.

"Everything the Avatar said is true, isn't it?" asked the Lieutenant. "I just saw you bloodbend her!"

Amon fixed his cruel gaze on his second-in-command but said nothing. The Lieutenant lowered his head. His worst fears had been confirmed. He stripped off his mask and dropped it to the ground, crushing it beneath his feet.

"You traitor! I dedicated my life to you!" the Lieutenant shouted. He charged Amon, pulling his kali sticks from his belt.

Amon snapped his head toward the Lieutenant and bloodbent him in midstep. With a twist of his arm, he jerked the Lieutenant's body into the air and hurled him across the room. The Lieutenant crashed into a stack of crates.

Korra stirred at the noise of the impact just as Mako managed to push himself to his knees. Amon turned to look at him, surprised that the Firebender had been able to move in his bloodbending grip.

He walked over to Mako, intent on finishing him, when suddenly a brilliant bolt of lightning exploded from the Firebender's body. The lightning struck Amon, blasting him off his feet. The Equalist leader flew through the air and smashed into the wall of the gym.

Now free of Amon's hold, Mako rushed over to Korra and picked her up in his arms. He carried her out of the gym and raced down the corridor.

"Mako . . . my bending," Korra said faintly.

"Everything will be all right. We just need to get out of here," he told her.

Just then, his body seized and Korra fell from his arms. Amon emerged from the opposite end of the hall, once again capturing Mako in his bloodbending grip. Mako's limbs twisted as Amon jerked his body back and forth, slamming him ruthlessly against the walls of the corridor.

Finally, Amon forced Mako to his knees in front of him.

"I'm impressed. No one has ever gotten the better of me like that. It is almost a shame to take the bending of someone so talented," Amon hissed. *"Almost."*

He fixed his hands on Mako's face and moved to take his bending.

From the other end of the hall, Korra felt frozen by helplessness, until a fury overtook her. The desire to save Mako burned brightly inside her, giving her the will to stop Amon.

"No!" she screamed. Instinctively, she threw a punch

and was shocked when a powerful wave of air surged from her fist. The gust blasted Amon away from Mako.

Korra's eyes grew wide. "I can airbend?" she asked in wonder.

"Impossible!" Amon snarled.

She drew herself up to her feet. "I can airbend!" Korra shouted. She threw another punch and sent a gust of wind spiraling down the corridor. Amon staggered under the strength of the blow.

Mako watched as Korra fought her way forward, pummeling Amon with fierce torrents of air. She drove him back to the window at the end of the hallway.

Amon stumbled, dropping to his knees. Korra moved to close the distance between them, but at the last moment, he reached out, clenching his fingers in the air.

Korra's body went rigid. She struggled in Amon's bloodbending grasp, but this time it felt different. She sensed the weakness in his grip and realized she could beat it.

"No. You. *Don't!*" Korra said through gritted teeth. She summoned her strength, and her leg snapped out in a fluid kick. An explosion of air surged from the kick, knocking Amon through the window. He tumbled through the air and fell into the bay, unconscious.

Korra pulled Mako to his feet and the two of them

ran to the broken window. They looked over the pier next to the arena and scanned the water. Amon's mask floated on the surface of the waves, but there was no sign of him.

The crowd of people on the pier glanced up at Korra and Mako. They had witnessed Amon's fall, and they were angry.

"What did you do to our leader?" a man shouted.

"Evil Avatar!" yelled a woman.

Suddenly, there was a rumbling in the bay. Beneath the waves, Amon came to, frightened to discover he was underwater. He choked as water spilled into his nose and mouth, and instinctively lashed out with waterbending. Amon sped toward the surface of the waves on a bubbling waterspout, which carried him high into the air.

The crowd on the pier gasped. Amon's secret was revealed.

"The Avatar was telling the truth!" cried an old man. Some in the crowd grumbled, while others whispered in small groups, but most of the Equalists fell into a stunned silence as they began to understand the enormity of Amon's lies. They had let themselves be fooled, and Republic City and many innocent people had paid a terrible price for their foolishness.

Korra stared hard at Amon as he floated on top of

the spinning whirlpool. The last of his "scars" from being attacked by a Firebender trickled from his face in streaks of colored water. They were nothing more than face paint.

Amon let the waterspout drop and fell back into the bay. Mako thought about pursuing him, slinging several jets of flame out over the water, but Amon was too quick. He rose and skimmed across the surface of the waves, headed for Air Temple Island.

Korra breathed a heavy sigh, but it wasn't exactly a sigh of relief. The war was over and Republic City was safe, but Amon had escaped. She'd finally been able to airbend after months of trying, only to lose her ability to control fire, water, and earth.

Exhausted, she leaned against Mako. He pulled her into his arms in a comforting hug, but it wasn't enough to silence the one thought that kept nagging at her: if she couldn't control all four elements, was she still the Avatar?

Tarrlok heard footsteps approaching and looked up through the bars of his prison cell. The trapdoor in the floor of the Air Temple's attic swung open. Amon climbed into the room—only it wasn't the Amon he was used to seeing. With the mask gone and the false scars removed from his face, Amon looked like someone Tarrlok hadn't seen in a very long time.

"Noatak," he said softly.

Amon walked slowly across the room and placed his hands on the bars of the cell. "It's over, brother. I'm sorry for what I had to do to you."

Tarrlok shook his head. "Our father set us on this path. Fate caused us to collide. I should have left with you when we were boys," he admitted.

Amon unlocked the door of the cell and pulled it open. "Leave with me now. We have a second chance. We can start over together." His voice dropped to a whisper. "*Please.* You're all I have left in the world."

Tarrlok gazed into his brother's face. Without the mask, Amon looked like a younger version of their father, and that was what worried him. Tarrlok sighed and stepped through the open cell door. This time, he decided to follow his brother. He couldn't help wondering, however, if there really was such a thing as a second chance.

36

It had taken a few days, but Republic City was finally on the mend. Equalist banners had been torn down, and buildings were being repaired after Amon's invasion. Commander Bumi and the second division of the United Forces had arrived, and under the leadership of General Iroh, they were helping to rebuild the city. But the most significant change came from the people themselves. Benders and non-benders worked alongside each other with the common goal of living together in peace.

Tenzin had rescued Pema, Beifong, and baby Rohan and returned to Air Temple Island with the rest of the family. There was a sense of hope in the air after Amon's defeat, but Korra found it hard to celebrate. Her powers still hadn't returned.

There was only one thing she could think to do, and that was return to the Southern Water Tribe lands where she'd trained to become the Avatar. She knew she'd find her waterbending master, Katara, Avatar Aang's widow and one of the best healers in the world.

Korra made the journey south along with Tenzin and his family. Mako, Bolin, Asami, and Beifong followed. Everyone was eager to see Korra healed.

Time seemed to crawl as they waited through the long healing session with waterbending master Katara.

Finally, Katara and Korra emerged. In the room where everyone had gathered to wait, Katara addressed her son Tenzin, her grandchildren, and all of Korra's friends and loved ones.

"I've tried everything in my power, but I cannot restore Korra's bending," she said sadly.

"But you're the best healer in the world. You have to keep trying!" Beifong pleaded.

"I'm sorry." Katara shook her head. "There's nothing else I can do. Korra can still airbend, but her connection to the other elements has been severed."

Tenzin walked over to Korra and put an arm around her shoulders. "It's going to be all right," he said.

Korra gave Tenzin a long, hard look. "No," she said miserably. "It's not." She grabbed her tunic and walked outside into the snow.

After a beat, Mako ran after her.

"Korra, wait!" he called.

Korra spun around to face him. "Go away," she said sullenly.

"I will, but I want you to know I'm here for you," Mako explained.

"No, I mean go away—back to Republic City! Get on with your life!" She folded her arms across her chest.

"What are you talking about?" he asked, hurt.

"I'm not the Avatar anymore." Korra bristled. "You don't need to do me any favors." She turned away from him.

"I don't care if you're the Avatar or not," Mako said. "Listen, when Tarrlok took you, I was losing my mind at the thought of never seeing you again." He took hold of her arm and turned her to face him. "I realized . . . I love you, Korra," he whispered.

Korra blinked as Mako stepped closer and placed a gentle hand on her cheek. Some part of her had been waiting to hear him say that from the first moment she'd met him, but that part of her no longer mattered. It was gone, along with her bending.

Korra shook her head and brushed his hand away. "I . . . can't," she said sadly. She backed away from him and ran off across the icy plateau.

Mako lowered his head, crushed. He was startled when he saw Tenzin walk up beside him.

"We need to be patient with her," Tenzin said. "It will take time for her to accept what has happened."

On a high-powered speedboat in the middle of the ocean, Amon and Tarrlok sped toward the horizon.

"The two of us together again . . . there's nothing we can't do," Amon told his brother.

Tarrlok studied his brother and the strange expression in his eyes. He glanced at the wooden crate of electrified gloves sitting next to him on the deck.

"Yes, Noatak," Tarrlok said softly.

"Noatak . . . I had almost forgotten the sound of my own name," Amon replied. He looked out over the bow into the setting sun in the distance.

"It will be just like old times," Tarrlok agreed. He pulled one of the Equalist gloves from the crate and slipped it on. Leaning over the side of the boat, Tarrlok found the gas tank and unscrewed the lid. He touched the glove to the open tank and took one last look at his brother, who was facing away from him.

He wanted to believe in second chances, but there was too much of their father in both of them for that.

Tarrlok triggered the glove and sparks shot into the gas tank.

From a distance, the explosion looked like nothing more than a brilliant burst of light. Anyone who saw it would never know that it marked the end of the sad tale of two ill-fated brothers.

Korra had no idea how long she'd wandered across the snow and ice. It felt as if she'd walked to the ends of the earth. She had definitely reached the end of the land, as the ground dropped off ahead of her in steep cliffs of ice.

Korra walked to the edge of the cliffs near the ocean and looked into the frigid water below. She felt a lot like that frozen sea—cold, alone, and at the very bottom of a great height. She sank to her knees and brushed the tears from her eyes. When she heard footsteps approaching, she didn't bother to look up.

"Not now, Tenzin. I just want to be left alone," she said.

"But you called me here." It wasn't Tenzin's voice.

Startled, Korra looked up quickly. A ghostly vision of Avatar Aang drifted in front of her. "Aang . . . ," Korra breathed in astonishment.

The Avatar nodded, his red and gold Airbender's robes swirling around him.

"You have finally connected with your spiritual self," he said.

"How?" she asked.

"When we reach our lowest point, we are open to the greatest change," Aang answered. Behind him, the air shimmered and a heavy mist fell over the sky. Figures rippled and emerged from the mist. Korra recognized them as the Avatars of the past. After Aang, there was Avatar Roku, then Avatar Kyoshi, and on and on, stretching back across the generations to the beginning of time.

The air hummed with the vibration of the Spirits, and the figure of Aang reached out to touch a single finger to Korra's forehead. His eyes glowed a brilliant white, which spilled over into the eyes of the Avatars behind him. Aang's arrow tattoos flared as the energy inside him, the energy of all the Avatars, shot through him into Korra.

Korra closed her eyes, feeling the heat of that energy envelop her. When she opened her eyes, they glowed with the same blinding white light. In the Avatar State, she rose into the air as the power coursed through her, sending a shock wave of air rippling across the plateau. A ring of fire formed on the ground beneath her. The earth rumbled, and then the waters of the frozen sea melted and crashed against the cliffs.

Korra sank back to the ground. Her powers were restored. When the light in her eyes faded, she noticed that Aang and the other Avatars were gone. Korra smiled. They weren't really gone. She was an avatar. They were always with her and she was always with them.

As Korra turned to make the long walk home, she saw Mako standing at the bottom of the slope leading away from the cliffs. He was staring at her in wonder and awe. She ran toward him, hoping it wasn't too late. When she reached him, she launched herself into his arms.

"I love you, too," she said.

Mako looked down at her with his lopsided grin. *Finally,* he thought.

Korra, too, was tired of waiting. She closed her arms around Mako's shoulders and kissed him.

With her powers returned to her, Korra knew that she could fix the damage done by Amon. As Aang had done for her, Korra would do for others. Working from a deep place within herself, she would share her power to restore bending to the people Amon had harmed. First among them was Lin Beifong, whose courage and bravery had saved her more than once.

Outside Katara's hut, Beifong knelt in front of Korra. Tenzin and his family looked on, along with Katara, Mako, Asami, and Bolin, as Korra reached out and gently touched a single finger to Beifong's forehead. The Avatar's eyes glowed as power coursed through her and traveled into Beifong's body. The former police chief drew in a deep breath as her connection to the earth was reestablished. The ground rumbled beneath her feet and she stood.

"Thank you," she said to the Avatar.

Korra bowed, the light in her eyes fading. It was strange, the combination of power and humility. Tenzin walked over to her, beaming with pride. When he'd taken on her training, he'd known she was special.

"I'm so proud of you, *Avatar* Korra," he said.

Korra smiled. For the first time, the title felt absolutely right. She liked how it sounded, and anyone who didn't . . . well, they would just have to deal with it.